WEDDING IN AUTUMN

AND OTHER STORES

S̲ʜɪʜ C̲ʜɪᴜɴɢ-Y̲ᴜ

WEDDING IN AUTUMN

AND OTHER STORES

Translated from the Chinese by

Darryl Sterk

BALESTIER PRESS
LONDON · SINGAPORE

Balestier Press
71-75 Shelton Street, London WC2H 9JQ
www.balestier.com

Wedding in Autumn and Other Stories
Copyright © Shih Chiung-Yu 1990, 1992, 1993

A collection of three novellas:
Wedding in Autumn
Original title: 秋天的婚禮
Flee, Ma-wu-k'u River
Original title: 奔逃, 馬武窟溪
The Last Whistling Pine, Forgotten by the Windbreak
Original title: 被林子遺忘的最後一株木麻黃

English translation copyright © Darryl Sterk 2018

First published by Balestier Press in 2018

A CIP catalogue record for this book
is available from the British Library.

ISBN 978 1 911221 01 2

Contents

Wedding in Autumn

7

Flee, Ma-wu-k'u River

33

The Last Whistling Pine, Forgotten by the Windbreak

59

Wedding in Autumn

"Ah Ju's back!" Ah Ju, the girl from the road crew dormitory. That's what we all called her, because that's where she grew up. She disappeared for a quite a while, but now she was back, and she brought two people with her: her fiancé, and her unborn child. I hadn't seen her pregnant belly yet, so I didn't know if it was a bump or a peak, if she was going to have a boy or a girl. But if there's one thing I did know, it's that women are unpredictable, and that the origin of a woman's erratic temper is her womb.

They chose to hold Ah Ju's wedding in October. Taiwanese people sure do like October weddings. My family gets quite a number of invitations every October. The festive designs on the invitations remind me of all the national flags flapping on every street corner at this time of year. October is a special month. The Wuchang Uprising was launched in October. Taiwan was returned to Chinese rule in October. Generalissimo Chiang Kai-shek was born in October, too. No surprise that lovers like to tie the knot in October. To me, it's almost like October is dyed different shades of red. Our national flag is a dignified red. The fireworks display set off at night on the Tenth of October is a dazzling red. The Cutex makeup October brides apply to their lips and nails is a cheerful red. The wedding invitations that bombard us in October are an irksome red. And I have seen another shade of red—thick and sticky and vital, throbbing imploringly, stiflingly raw on the scorching sandy ground. It gurgled out of Ah Ju's groin, scaled the fallen leaves of the horsetail she-oak trees, spread beseechingly towards me, but soon seeped into the sandy soil, drawing a final panicked breath as I turned tail and ran.

If I hadn't seen that shudder-inducing shade of red, I think I would have replied more eagerly when my dad asked me to attend Ah Ju's wedding on his behalf. Actually, I don't mind attending wedding receptions at all, for my own not altogether honourable reasons.

My family had three weddings to attend on the same day. There my father stood, looking down at a pile of October wedding invitations. He could make it, he said, to the two banquets that were close by. "Why don't you attend the girl from the road crew dormitory's reception on our behalf?" My dad isn't too good at giving orders. He says we already have one Fascist in the family, which is why he's always been Mr Nice Guy, even though he's a local official, a County Councillor. But if he'd actually ordered me to go, I might have refused him outright. What Dad is good at is whining: "They never have anything I feel like eating. Not that I ever get the chance to eat with all the toasting. I always get woozy when I drink, and my finicky stomach will act up for days afterwards. But if I don't go people will say I'm—" Tired of listening to his litany of muttered complaints, I just cut him off in mid-sentence: "All right! I'll go!"

Actually, just like I said, I don't much mind attending wedding banquets. There's often something in it for me, you know: I get a piece of the action. Of course, if it's a thousand dollar bill, it's more complicated. I have to break it into five hundreds and hundreds so I can pocket part of the sum. Nobody'll know, and what they don't know won't hurt them. In any case, my family isn't going to hold a banquet when me and my sister get married (you know what I mean): my dad says he doesn't want to inflict the obligation of the red envelope on anyone, so we'll just keep things simple. Which means we're never going to get even with all the people that invited us to their wedding banquets. I reckon that by stealing a few bills from the red envelope I can reduce the pain, keep part of the money in the family. But then one time my mother got it into her head to give a plaque instead: "Your colleagues on the County Council give wooden plaques with proverbs on them. It saves money, and the family likes it. Why don't we just do that?" That time there was no proverbial oil for me to skim. I had to go to the ceremony carrying this plaque. But, strange to say, my mum was right: the family made more of a fuss over the plaque than anyone had ever done over a red envelope. They gathered round me and the plaque and shouted: "Hang it up! Hang it up! Councillor's son!"

So they chose to hold Ah Ju's wedding in autumn. Strange that Ah Ju would wait until she was big with child before getting hitched. My mother said that her and her fiancé had been living together, but I still thought it was strange. Especially since I assumed she was the hen that wouldn't lay any more eggs. How'd she managed to get herself pregnant again?

I decided Ah Ju's womb would be forever barren when we were reading Chapter 14 in health education class. It was a morning in early autumn. I'd woken up to the sound of a rooster crowing and our hunting dog and wolfhound barking. Ah Ju was carrying a big rooster by the feet and leading her blind father, Uncle Chu, by the arm. The bird spread its wings wide, struggling upside-down in Ah Ju's clutches and leaving a roomful of feathers floating in the air. Our hunting dog Ding Ding found its weird clucking less than euphonious, bared his teeth and growled after his own strange fashion.

"Cownsler, this heeere's fer you." Supporting himself on his cane, Uncle Chu motioned for Ah Ju to give the fat rooster to my mother. "We raised 'im ussselves. He's a jenuwine Tah-wan rooster."

I sat up under the covers and peeked through the crack in the door. Ah Ju was wearing a belted white dress with black polka dots. She looked haggard. Her eyes were all puffy, looking even smaller than they usually did. I bet she was pregnant again. Folks say that a pregnant lady is the most beautiful she'll ever be in her life, but Ah Ju just seemed emaciated. And her family had to give us a chicken every time she had a bun in the oven. This was the third one. Uncle Chu looked really worried.

"I still want 'er to wed. Doctor says, if she has another one taken out she'll never have a baby again."

"Is it the boy in the coastal defence again?" asked my mother, using the Taiwanese idiom for the coast guard.

"That's the one! It'll be the end of me. He doesn't have to want our Ah Ju, but does he have to spoil 'er like this?" Ah Ju just stood there, hanging her head. I couldn't see the look on her flat face. She was probably expressionless, actually, her eyes dazed or even a bit dull. Expressionless was about the only expression Ah Ju ever wore.

"Are you talking about the boy from the west coast? The same one as before?" my father asked, looking at my mum— Dad doesn't understand Taiwanese too well (he grew up in China). "Is he willing to do the honourable thing?"

"Same old excuse. He says he's just a poor recruit, without a penny to his name."

"What did he say?" said my dad. My mum translated from Taiwanese to Mandarin and my dad asked: "Then what does his family say?"

"They say he's his own man, and that they can't afford for him to take a wife!" said Uncle Chu.

Ah Ju was a bit of a dolt to begin with, and now she'd got knocked up a few times without ever finding a man who wanted to marry her. All Uncle Chu could do was stand behind her, and help her clean up the mess. He was living off his savings from a dozen years in the road crew and waiting for Ah Ju to find a good man, even though she was just an adopted daughter he'd purchased from a poor family. Uncle Chu had come to my father to ask him to mediate several times on account of the scandal of Ah Ju's inflamed womb. Everyone was used to Ah Ju's blunders. "Yeah! That's Tits for you!" folks would say, shaking their heads. A few got quite worked up over Ah Ju, no one more than Miss Sensitive, my elder sister Min-teh. Every time Min-teh heard about Ah Ju's exploits she would clench her arms in front of her chest, grind her teeth and say: "Has Ah Ju lost every brain cell she ever had?!"

I couldn't understand why Min-teh got so upset. It reminded me of how she sounded talking about taking part in the Child Prostitute Rescue Parade up in Taipei. I think maybe she'd got the wrong idea, and taken Ah Ju for a whore. It wasn't like that at all. Ah Ju was willing, all right. She didn't take money; heck, it looked like she wanted it so bad maybe she should have had to pay for it.

Ah Ju and Min-teh used to be elementary classmates, and now they're both in their early twenties. Min-teh has gone abroad to study, while Ah Ju's had a hard life: she got knocked up and dumped several times, and here she is pregnant again and about to get married. People's fates really are thousands of miles apart, even when they grow up in the same place. I never realized that before; I guess I'm growing up.

Later on the bad romance between Ah Ju and the swine of a coast guard recruit just fizzled out. God knows where she got the courage, but she went to the west coast for a while and I heard this trip home she's got a lot more savvy and feisty. Now she understands how people talk dirt about her, and apparently she gives as good in return. But it's still unclear to me and everyone else why she didn't get married a few months back, when her belly wasn't so big. It's just that with Ah Ju being so savvy and all, nobody dares to ask.

The stupid things Ah Ju did back then seem in retrospect like a ridiculous movie played in reverse. Ah Ju was the heroine of the farce. Maybe "heroine" isn't the right word, seeing as how she was the one who made a fool of herself. At the time

I was too young to play the role of the leading man, and I've come to realize I was always playing the same bit part. I never got a single line, and the only chance I had to change roles, I got stage fright. As I've already told you, I freaked out and fled the scene.

Ah Ju was never a pretty girl. Her appearance was like all those stupid things she did a few years back, less than appealing. But even so there've been quite a few men in her life, more than any other girl in the village. Back in the day, Ah Ju's best quality was that she was obedient. She never talked much or showed her feelings, but if you told her to do something, she'd grunt and do it for you. Uncle Chu's colleagues in the road crew, old geezers from the Mahjong gazebo, and even little brats playing in the mud got into the habit of ordering her around:

"Ah Ju, go buy me a pack of cigarettes at the store."

"Ah Ju, get me a bucket of water."

"Ah Ju, Ah Ju, I want a lollipop, go get me one, pretty pleeeeease!"

Ah Ju rarely said no. Of course one reason was that she hardly said anything, and even when she spoke, she mumbled, like her voice was stuck in her throat. Ah Ju's face was angular and thin, but also flat, and her slitty eyes were suspended in that flat face of hers. She always looked enervated, like she hadn't slept enough. When she did speak, her thin dry lips would pout outward and expose two rows of narrow, uneven teeth, through which her voice sluiced indistinctly. If you edged closer to her tiny oral cavity to hear better, you might smell organic matter (stuck in the gaps between her teeth) rotting on her breath.

But when Uncle Chu's cataracts got so bad that he was basically blind, Ah Ju started talking more.

"Step up. Again. Good!"

"Taxi's here. Give me your cane. Get in."

"Open your mouth. Today it's tilapia with rice."

"Watch out! There's a dog turd up ahead."

Uncle Chu chose the right time to go blind, the first year after Ah Ju graduated from elementary school. Ah Ju didn't continue to junior high, so she could spend the whole day taking care of old Uncle Chu. Ah Ju would hold his arm as he tap tapped his way along with his cane, like a daughter at her daddy's side. People who saw them would drop whatever they were doing. Oh it's too bad about Uncle Chu: what good has it done him to save all this money now that he's too blind to see anything? Or they'd praise Ah Ju for being so filial, treating Uncle Chu like her own flesh and blood: "Ah Ju is an obedient child."

After Uncle Chu grew accustomed to his blindness, and learned how to take care of himself, Ah Ju went to help at the sundry goods shop "Big Sis" that Ah Tao operated. Around that time Ah Ju changed fast. And I mean fast. You might find it hard to believe that I was too much of a kid (kid's not the right word—I was older than a kid, but not quite a teenager) to know the significance of the sudden change that had come upon her. In the past few years, I have experienced a growth spurt myself, along with all the other changes that come with puberty. But at the time I was shocked: it seemed like someone had worked magic upon Ah Ju, giving her a strange aura, a kind of provocative ambiance. It was a feeling I couldn't imagine getting from my elder sister Min-teh. It was a kind of hazy beauty intellectual girls like Miss Sensitive are bereft of. Intellect deprives women of their feminine qualities. And my elder sister has been an intellectual ever since she was a little girl. I'll never forget how the alarm would ring at six o'clock every morning, time for her to get up, rummage around for her glasses, and then start reciting English sentence patterns: "Tom is my classmate, Eamon is my friend." She'd wake me up with the sound of her chanting (I had the rotten luck of having to share a room with her: she slept on the bottom bunk, I slept on the top), and then enunciate: "'Stupid' means dumb. And 'pig' is what you look like if you look like Ah Chung." Ah Chung is my name! Tell me, how was anyone supposed to see feminine mystery in a girl like that?

One day, she was in the bathroom wailing: "Mum! My MC has come." Min-teh was such a know-it-all in those days. She was just bleeding, wasn't she? Why'd she need to call it her Menstrual Cycle, like it was Science class or something? When I learned the secret, that she was bleeding from her behind, I couldn't help staring, like it was some kind of paranormal phenomenon. Min-teh was so pale I even started worrying she might pass out. So it took me completely by surprise when she blew up at me: she kicked me in the groin as hard as she could and shrieked: "What are you looking at? Huh? Don't be so smug. The same is in store for you. You know what a wet dream is? Pretty soon you'll have to wear a nappy to bed. Can you imagine it? Ah Chung in a nappy! You wait and see!"

I was rolling around on the floor clutching my balls, unable to breathe. I can't help wondering whether she was responsible for the hernia operation I had when I was ten. She used to kick me when Mum wasn't looking. Had she kicked my guts through my abdominal wall? You get the idea: Min-teh was an ever so slightly imperious girl who threw temper tantrums. It was impossible to imagine a girl (or woman?) like that displaying feminine qualities. Ah Ju was different. She was a lot dumber. But she was feminine in a way I was more easily able to understand. Around her, at least, I never had to defend myself.

Ah Ju's qualities were mysterious, but on full display. I could stand a few metres outside the sundry goods shop and smell her as she worked quietly and diligently inside, fine beads of sweat forming on her thin and nimble hands. In a warm breeze of early summer, I'd go walking past Ah Tao's shop and hear Ah Tao yelling at Ah Ju to do things, and Ah Ju responding woodenly: "Mmmm." There were baskets of eggs, bottles of cola and wooden crates, and the sun sprinkled down onto a display of sweet jars. Ah Ju would often stand by that display wrapping betel nut, and every time I would smell hints of wet heat in the air. Were the eggs rotten? Was there mildew in the crates? I wasn't sure. So I asked my friends Ah Ma Lung and Ah Hsin Chung to help me work it out.

"Smells like a bitch in heat!" Ah Ma said, sniffing.

"It's basically BO, but stronger. That means Ah Ju is a total skank!" said Ah Hsin, holding his nose as he walked towards the door of the shop, until big fat Ah Tao had a go at him: "Buy something or beat it, you little beast!"

Soon I was sure that was Ah Ju's smell. With the warmth of an early summer breeze, Ah Ju started wearing a pastel summer dress with coffee coloured stains, and her newly budding breasts were like protuberant brown eyes, sticking out silently and secretly, insistently pendant in the chest of her faded dress. Standing outside, I could always hear Ah Ju working. She didn't talk much. But I was vaguely conscious that she had her own way of communicating. With those two brown eyes. With that smell that was none too elegant but nonetheless arresting, wafting from who knows what body part. But who was she communicating with? Can't be me, I thought.

Later I learned who it was. Ah Tao's baby brother went to help out at the store, too. His eyes were dark and bright, and his face was like a tasty apple pie. He'd been at a loose end since graduating from junior high. He was handsome and fair, refined and clean. He wore a white T-shirt and faded jeans every day. I couldn't understand how a guy like that, so crisp and smart, would leave school after finishing junior high, or how someone so good-looking could click with a girl like Ah Ju. Everyone was so surprised when Ah Ju started showing, like a river bursting its banks. Everyone, that is, but me: I knew their secret.

Ah Tao's little brother smelled Ah Ju, too. He keened to her secret body language, and then he just reached out his hands. He really did. He rolled up his sleeves, revealing a shy fuzz on his comely, glistening arms, the veins concealed by youth. He sensed Ah Ju's subtle monologue in the air of the shop, and made a timely response. I saw it with my own eyes. He'd been working around the shop, and then his hands settled on Ah Ju's protuberant brown eyes and started petting them, or polishing them, like he was polishing a precious gem. All that polishing must have generated heat, because the two of them retreated behind the red curtain at the back of the shop to cool off. The sultry southern breeze blew, and the corners of the curtain began to sway. They kept swaying until Ah Ju got pregnant. But that handsome, shy younger brother of Ah Tao's was all of sixteen years old. Should they get married or not?

Ah Tao's brother ended up leaving for the big city to learn to be an electrician or a plumber or something, while that unformed foetus in Ah Ju's belly disappeared somehow. I think that must have been Ah Tao's doing.

"Ah Ju really was in heat," said Ah Ma, winding up his bat over the sandy pitch outside the coast guard, with one of his old man's President-brand cigarettes dangling from his mouth. "Ah Ju must have seduced Ah Di. How could such a handsome guy see anything in her?"

"How do you know she seduced him?" I wasn't trying to speak up for Ah Ju, just curious to know whether Ah Ma, who was usually so inattentive, had discovered the secret, too.

"Take a look at her chest and you'll see," Ah Ma said.

"What?"

"Next time you pass the shop, take a good look at her ta-tas. There are two dark pegs just waiting for you to hang your hands on." Ah Ma and Ah Hsin exchanged a look and sniggered.

Ah Ju kept helping out around the shop. Summer left and winter came and the two protuberant orbs on her chest were bundled up in a coat with cotton padding. Come spring, Ah Ju's eyes seemed to open again after a long hibernation, shining more brightly than ever. I thought Ah Ma and Ah Hsin would have to think of a new word. A peg was too small, too thin. Mushroom? As soon as Ah Ma and Ah Hsin said it they couldn't stop laughing. "Do you want some mushroom, Ah Chung?" Mushroom was much better. It was like a little mound in the distance, soft and plump.

Ah Ju was working in the sundry goods shop, in her usual diligent, quiet way. She'd always fulfil customer requests promptly, then continue to leaf the betel nut. When Ah Ju bent over, those two mushrooms of hers drooped gently upon the fabric of her dress, and the upside-down peak of each protuberance was even more pronounced. Next time my mum made mushrooms for dinner, I couldn't help it: I curled up in my chair in silent mirth.

It was right around then that the coast guard got a troop of raw recruits. The procurement sergeant chose Ah Tao's shop, and would spend the longest time there with a team of recruits, because the proprietresses of the other shops were old and ugly. Ah Ju wasn't exactly pretty, but at least she was young. I'd heard that when guys go into the military they turn into pigs. And the coast guard boys who helped buy supplies would surround Ah Ju and flirt with her and generally behave like beasts: they told dirty jokes that weren't funny at all, and then laughed themselves silly, while Ah Ju would just hang her head and smile. You never knew whether she got the joke, because she was always smiling, no matter what. The recruits offered her lots of invitations, and she didn't nod or say no. One square-faced fellow with a nose like a clove of garlic and skin like pig flesh laughed and said: "Not saying no means yes!

Where's a good place for a date around here?"

Ah Ju actually started seeing the vicious swine. Ah Ma, Ah Hsin and me would be playing baseball on the sand by the coast guard barracks, and there was Ah Ju off work, leaning on the wall topped by glass shards, waiting for her lover, the biggest pig private of them all. He'd come out, sweating furiously and wearing a stinky white singlet and a pair of red shorts slit high. He'd reach out and take Ah Ju by her delicate waist and lead her into the horsetail she-oaks in the dense windbreak; then we'd put aside the game we were playing and follow them with our eyes until they disappeared into the depth and darkness of the grove. "When a bitch is in heat, she'll do it with anyone," said Ah Ma, with the solemnity of a wise man. (Do what? I thought.) Then we'd finish playing our game. After not so long, maybe half an hour (none of us had brought a watch), we'd see the private and Ah Ju come walking out of the grove, and we'd put our game aside another time to stare at them. Sometimes the ball would slide under the private's thick and solid legs, and he would say: "Whacha lookin' at? Never seen it before? You little runts ain't got no manners. Get rollin'!" Or something like that. He'd toss our ball back over, and I was never sure if it was us he wanted to get rolling or the ball.

Ah Ju came to the coast guard really, really often, so often that Ah Ma and Ah Hsin got tired of telling the jokes about pegs or mushrooms. We'd keep playing ball, listening to what they were doing in the windbreak. Occasionally we'd hear the private shout like a crazed beast in that rough, ugly voice of his: "Fuck yer mama! I'll kill ya! See if I don't!" Or, in a different tone of voice: "I'll make ya cum! You'll cum so hard!"

I didn't understand why the pig yelled at Ah Ju in such a nasty way, or why she never talked back. I wanted to sound cool or wise like Ah Ma when I said: "At least Ah Ju should tell him: 'Fuck yer mama's cunt!' in return." The C word was so nasty. It sure hadn't been easy to say; my folks never let me use profanity. I thought Ah Ma and Ah Hsin would applaud my awesome insult, but they seemed unimpressed. Ah Ma put his mouth close to my ear and said: "Ah Chung, I'll tell you a secret."

"What's that?"

"You're a complete moron." What? A moron?

At first I assumed Ah Ma and Ah Hsin stopped telling jokes about pegs and mushrooms because they were tired of them, but then I discovered that at some point they'd turned against Ah Ju. "Ah Ju's a 'ho.' Anyone can have his way with her. Anyone." "Ah Chung, don't buy stuff from Ah Tao's shop any more. Aren't you worried about getting sick if you eat something Ah Ju's touched?" Ah Ma and Ah Hsin warned me. Every day after school when the line passed by the shop, Ah Ma and Ah Hsin would spit and say: "Bitch!" "Slut!" But when Ah Ju was really in trouble, they stood up for her, and spoke up on her behalf.

The fiery red sun was sinking behind the tips of the she-oak trees. We were on the sandy ground near the gate to the coast guard barracks, playing our last game of ball before dinner. As usual, Ah Ju was off work, her backside tucked in a gap in the pile of firewood by the wall, waiting for her swinish lover, who didn't pay her much attention anymore. He came out, his brutish face needing a bat to the head I thought, and as soon as he saw Ah Ju he lost his temper and said: "Didn't Ah tell ya not to come round here no more?" He turned and walked a few steps, then looked back and saw Ah Ju hadn't moved a muscle. She was still looking at him with a dazed expression in her tiny eyes. That pissed him off even more: "Whaddya want? I told ya. I'm not going to marry ya. So what the fuck do ya want?"

Ah Ju never replied, just stared woodenly at her swinish loverboy, with no sadness in her eyes. She squatted on the dry wood pile, the hem of her dress covering her skinny lower body, her right hand ceaselessly peeling the bark of the dried she-oak logs beneath her bum and tossing the peels on the sandy ground.

"Roll on home! Quit harassin' me!" Before he got on his way, he added: "Fuck yer mama! Since when did my luck turn so bad?" Then he picked up a rock and tossed it at her. Who knows where he found the courage, but Ah Ma walked over and stood in front of the guy, who seemed many times bigger than he, looked up and said: "Hey! You think we easterners are easy to push around? You're the one who should roll on home!"

"Ho ho ho, look who's talking!" laughed the private in a creepy voice. "You talk pretty big for such a little guy. Must be a little big man!" Then he used his right index finger to push Ah Ma on the head, hard, a couple of metres away. Then it was Ah Hsin's turn to say in a high-pitched, trembling voice that was loud and clear: "Hey, you smelly westerner! My dad was a commander in the civil war. He fought the commies before you were even born. I'll get him to tell your superiors what you've been up to. They'll put you in solitary!"

I was scared speechless, especially when the pig started laughing his head off.

"If yer daddy was a commander, then I was the President of the ROC. Ya little shit!"

Ah Ma gathered up the bat, gloves and balls and said: "Let's go home." When we passed Ah Ju, Ah Ma petulantly spat on the ground and said: "Bitch!" Ah Hsin did the same. When it was my turn I took a look at Ah Ju, who was staring blankly, her hands covered in wood shavings. I didn't say a thing. Actually, what I wanted to say was: "Come on home, Ah Ju."

This time Ah Ju didn't wait until her belly got all swollen up before getting rid of it. And this time people assumed Ah Ju would wise up, and give up on her brutish beau, but she didn't. She kept coming to wait for him outside the gate by the windbreak after work. Having had two abortions, Ah Ju seemed headed for an early decline, which didn't reconcile with her juvenile manner. She looked like a world-weary middle-aged woman. She didn't take care of herself, didn't dress up or put on makeup. Her hair was thin to begin with, and when she tied it into a ponytail with an elastic band there were always stray wisps at the nape of her neck. Her dress was just old, stained, trailing loose threads, with a rusty zip. But she acted so naive, like she had no idea how the world works. The private would come out and see her, every once in a while, and it was like she'd never wondered whether or not she'd get to see her loverboy tonight, or what his attitude towards her actually was. Going to wait by the gate every day seemed part of her daily routine. I used to see her squatting on the pile of firewood absentmindedly pulling almost all the bark off the logs, or kicking the sand into a little pile, a pretty little hill.

The private would come out and see her and promptly forget he'd ever got her up the spout. He couldn't wait to stick his hand up her shirt, and take her into the bushes. But when he was done he seldom forgot to remind Ah Ju not to come and bother him ever again.

The third time she got pregnant, Uncle Chu brought Ah Ju and the private to our house to negotiate again. How could she keep getting pregnant in such a short time? It was over my head, because I didn't have a womb. Ah Ju's complexion got increasingly pale on account of all the pregnancies, because her womb was sucking up all the sustenance she put into her body. Women's wombs are strange places: they can nourish new life and discharge it, over and over again. In that respect, a womb's kind of like my big sister's temper. One moment she'd say she wanted to play house or hopscotch, the next minute she'd be whacking my head with the wooden spoon saying she'd never speak to me again. Soon she'd forget all about being angry and say: "Ah Chung, want to play again?"

Overall, nobody was satisfied with the result of the negotiation. Last time the pig had paid for the procedure in the end, but he was adamant he wasn't going to marry her. He couldn't raise a kid. He'd said: "Yeah, it's not like I don't want to do what's right. But how can I, eh? I'm in the coast guard now. I can't work. My old mama's the only family I got. Where am I s'posed to get money to support a child? And you can't blame it all on me. I told Ah Ju not to come round any more, I told her no girl who's sweet on me is ever going to be happy, but did she listen? She kept on coming to see me, every chance she got!"

Ah Ma said: "No surprise he wouldn't marry Ah Ju. Ah Ju's a broken shoe. Who'd want her? The doctor said, 'If Ah Ju has this abortion, she'll probably never bear a child again.' I heard the doctor even got angry with Ah Ju. 'How could you make a habit of having abortions?!'"

Now I've got to tell you what happened to the baby in her belly, which happens to be the reason why I don't want to go to Ah Ju's wedding reception.

Ah Ju continued to make the hike from the village to the gate. And there she would wait. That evening, as usual, I took my bat and mitt and was on my way to hit the ball on the sandy pitch. As I made my way through the windbreak, the setting sun was getting sieved through the foliage of the horsetail she-oaks. Funny that the sun in October could scorch the sand just as well as in summer, burning the bottoms of my flip-flops. A warm wind of autumn was blowing, still too warm to cool the sand down, a wind which would only blow in the south-western corner of the island. But what I saw in the windbreak that day was anything but typical: on the sand, scattered all around, were ruddy clots of bloody mucus, hot on the sand, raw under the sun. The smell reminded me of this one time when we let Ding Ding off his chain. He barked ferociously, and chased the chickens around the yard. One of those chickens, too fat to fly, met a terrible fate: Ding Ding snapped its neck, and carried it away, then came home, tail between his legs. I followed the droplets of blood all the way to the windbreak.

This time the trail of blood didn't lead to a dead chicken but to Ah Ju, who was sitting there miserably in a pool of her own blood. It was gruesome! Ah Ju was bleeding from her bum, like my sister Min-teh. But there was a huge amount of blood, and I mean huge. It was all over Ah Ju's skirt and legs, and it gave off a raw stench. She was holding her tummy with one hand, and supporting herself on the sand with the other. Her hands and fingernails were covered in fine sand and bloodstains. Was she in pain? It was certainly possible. Her flat face was contorted, and her eyes were scrunched into slits. Min-teh definitely hurt when she bled from her bum. She used to hole herself up in bed and roll around and cry, even when there were just a few small splotches of blood on her clothes. Most of the blood was absorbed by her Dependable tampons, which she used to toss in the bin in the bathroom. By contrast, Ah Ju was covered in gore.

I stopped and stared. Ah Ju's head was hanging, and her back was bowed. I forgot to tell you about her chest. Her mushrooms had morphed into jiggly, soft-cooked eggs, sunny-side up, the latest display of her secret fleshy ambiance, but I never knew that much blood could flow out of a woman's body. I was stunned. "Stunned" has been my excuse, my attempt to release myself from a sense of guilt that has haunted me ever since. In addition to being stunned, I recall three other impressions.

First, "Dirty." A woman's period was the waste product of her metabolism or something, and that waste had crawled all over Ah Ju's unclean body. I had an indescribable sense of disgust.

Second, "You're not a woman, so mind your own business." Whenever my sister Min-teh started bleeding there was a step she had to take, to gang up on me with Mother and consign me to the storage shed, where I would sleep on the dusty floor among heaps of stuff, with spiders' webs all around. A woman's business was her own; but no matter how stupid Ah Ju was, I thought, there's no way she should have got herself in this kind of trouble.

It was at this point my own neurosis kicked in, the consequence of the trauma Min-teh had inflicted upon me. I'd been worried my sister was going to die a pale death, so deathly white she was on account of all the blood flowing out of her behind, and she'd given me that nasty kick. I'd not forgotten. It was excruciating, the pain rising up from my abdomen. Oh no, I thought. I can't let anything like that happen again.

Third was Ah Ju's expression. As you've probably gathered, Ah Ju must have been sending out an SOS when I hightailed it out of there. I couldn't make the appointment to play ball with Ah Ma and Ah Hsin. I raced home, a heavy stone weighing upon my heart. When I got there, I hid myself in the shed and pretended to be asleep, but all I could think about was the expression on Ah Ju's face, which I'd seen the moment before leaving. It was the first time I'd ever seen her flat face expressive. It was as if a wooden mannequin had been given life.

That evening, I was called awake out of fitful sleep. My family had all eaten dinner. I wasn't hungry, but I tried to eat anyway. I shovelled cold leftovers into my mouth as I listened to my parents and Min-teh shooting the breeze in the cool of the front yard.

"I'll choose a few fat chickens when I go and see Ah Ju tomorrow morning. She'll need something wholesome to help her recover her health."

"Ah Ma and Ah Hsin are usually such slippery customers, but when someone really needed their help they did the right thing. It was big of them."

"Yeah, when they carried Ah Ju to the clinic they didn't know how long she'd been unconscious in the windbreak. The blood on her clothes was long dry. She'd been left for dead. If it hadn't been for them, Ah Ju might not have survived."

"This time that private is off the hook. He won't have to make any excuses. He won't even have to pay to get the baby out of Ah Ju's belly. It looks like Ah Ju is just not a lucky girl! She's never known who her parents are, and now she'll never have children of her own. She has no flesh and blood, and maybe nobody'll ever want her. The only good that's come of it is having that man out of her life. He never would have made her happy."

"Even if she had wanted to keep it, her womb has been scraped out so many times she would have lost it sooner or later."

"I just can't understand how she could be so stupid, going back to a guy who didn't want her. Mum and Dad, let me tell you, if a boy ever insulted me like that, I'd fix him so he'd never be able to carry on the family name: I'd cut his balls off!"

"Min-teh, girls shouldn't say such things."

"A miscarriage is never easy to recover from. I still think we should take Ah Ju—"

"Waaaaaa!"

I think I must have given my family quite a scare when I burst into tears, or they wouldn't have rushed into the house to see what was the matter. My mouth, expanded to several times its original size, was stuffed with sour tasting rice that I wasn't able to chew, but which somehow was no impediment to the volume of my cries. All I knew was that I was a sinner who'd refused to help Ah Ju in the moment of her direst need. I'd left her on death's door. The reeking bloody mass that oozed out of Ah Ju's groin was actually the last foetus that would ever form in her womb. And this innocent life had died, almost taking its mother with it.

That anguished cry of remorse hadn't completely died down when Ah Ju reappeared, miraculously pregnant, and planning on getting married.

*

They chose to hold Ah Ju's wedding in October. October's a holiday season, and a wedding season, too. We received three invitations for the day Ah Ju got married, and I was assigned to Ah Ju's event. My parents kept complaining about getting bombarded with wedding invitations, but they were especially generous to Ah Ju. They gave her a "Match of the Century" plaque and a thick red envelope. Now that I think of it, everyone was happy that Ah Ju had found someone to spend the rest of her life with and that she was still able to have a baby. Obviously nobody'd forgotten about all the stupid things Ah Ju did a few years back.

Ah Ju's wedding was just like any other: noisy and boisterous. They put up a temporary awning that shaded part of the courtyard, and brought over a dozen round tables and stools; and the cook set up his stove off to one side. The catering staff kept bringing out apparently tasty dishes that people just didn't feel like eating. The flies came, too, buzzing over our table. But at least in autumn, there was a coolness in the air. It would have been torture in summer, under a plastic awning, with everyone eating and sweating. We would have had to keep moving to avoid the direct light as the sun made its way across the sky. Anyway, the folks at the festive event weren't there to fill their bellies, but to eat a meal that would complete the ritual of marriage.

Ah Ju was not a beautiful bride. But thick makeup almost gave her a new face, a face that was painted red. There were red ribbons in her gelled hair. She was wearing pink eye shadow with sprinkles. Her cheeks were flushed scarlet. Her lips were a gorgeous red, her nails a soft vermillion. Her wedding dress was red, of course, a dark and brownish hue. And her belly was conspicuously bulging. Ah Ju's fiancé was a short guy, even shorter than Ah Ju, and he was bald. He must have been quite a bit older than her, though Ah Ju looked about ten years older than her actual age. The man had a genial air. He appeared satisfied and proud, and he smiled a toothy smile. Uncle Chu was smiling, too, no less toothily and proudly. He was in high spirits.

When Ah Ju came round to toast our table, Ah Ma and Ah Hsin were telling dirty jokes they'd heard in the military. What I'd feared as an adolescent had come to pass: the army had turned both of them into out-and-out swine. I was a bit sad, but also a bit curious to hear Ah Ma and Ah Hsin brag about their exploits in the "military paradise" on Quemoy Island.

Ah Ma said: "That one I always have to do her from behind, and she, well, she just crawls around on the ground like a dog, with her arse in the air. Ha ha ha! I give her a thrust, another thrust, and she starts barking like a dog. Christ! Friggin' doggy-style! It's sweet."

"Ah Ma, that's nothing. There's this young one, and every time she sees me it's like she hasn't had any for ages. She doesn't care it's not ladylike or demure or whatnot, she just yanks down my fly, he he he," said Ah Hsin.

When Ah Ju leaned close, I found it wasn't just her face that had changed. She was a completely different woman. She actually put her hand on Ah Hsin's shoulder, pressed a plastic cup of booze against Ah Ma's face and started joking around: "Ah Ma! Why didn't you ever make a move on me? If you had, it'd be you I'd be getting married to today." After her last toast, she would go and change outfits, as brides at weddings in Taiwan always did. But then it was like she remembered something. She reached out her bony fingers and fondled my head and said: "Ah Chung, how many years has it been? You're getting so big!"

She really had changed completely, in every way. Women were unpredictable. Ah Ju's transformation must have left me a bit dazed.

Ah Ma and Ah Hsin had finished with the dirty jokes and were now toasting like there was no tomorrow.

"You have to learn how to drink. Otherwise how're you going to survive in the military?" said Ah Ma.

"Yeah, don't be so strait-laced, you're killing me! What'll you do when it's your turn to do a tour of duty?" asked Ah Hsin.

The others at the table saw us playing drinking games and laughed. It wasn't like I didn't want to drink; but I couldn't forget the last time I'd gone to a reception. People kept toasting me, and I wasn't going to refuse, until I barfed all over the table, embarrassing my father and disgusting all the wedding guests. Maybe because they'd heard I couldn't hold my drink, Ah Ma and Ah Hsin weren't too keen on getting me drunk, and soon the conversation switched to Ah Ju's belly. Ah Ma bet she was going to have a boy, and Ah Hsin was sure it was going to be a girl. I wanted to place my own bet, but I felt sick to my stomach: a nasty gas was gurgling around in my gut. I left my seat and went to find the bathroom, holding my breath.

Ah Ju's house was dark, except for one room in which a yellowish lamp was lit. The door to the room was half open. And I saw Ah Ju inside, changing her clothes. It was the first time I'd ever seen a woman's body in my entire life.

Ah Ju unzipped the back of her dark red wedding dress, which seemed warm under the yellowish light, and slipped it off. Her naked shoulders were thin, accentuating the fullness of her breasts. Pegs, mushrooms, eggs cooked sunny-side up now seem ugly, rough figures of speech for her bosom. No, her breasts were limpid and luminous, like eyes, like an instinctive speech, like a dialogue of desire. Ah Ju slipped the sleeves off her arms, and pulled her dress down, until—

Whoosh—I thought I was letting out a smelly fart, but it turned out I'd lost control of my bowels. I actually shat my pants!

Ah Ju unwrapped the white strap around her waist, revealing a flawless hemisphere of fabric, like a pillow, which she shook out, parting the dusty air. Then, with a practised hand, she folded the fabric into a perfect half globe and, very carefully, like she was caressing a tiny infant, placed it upon her belly, and wrapped herself up again.

The cheongsam she changed into was also red. Would you believe me if I told you my eyes blurred? The clots of blood upon the sandy ground finally dissolved, and when my vision cleared, I saw the reddest flowers upon Ah Ju's Chinese-style wedding dress.

While in the air the stink of diarrhoea hung.

There'll be many other weddings in autumn.

But my dad won't ever let me go to another one.

As for Ah Ju's breasts, well, I finally saw them.

They were hundreds of times more beautiful than I'd imagined.

And as for Ah Ju's erratic womb, I never managed to figure out what was going on in there.

Did you?!

Flee, Ma-wu-k'u River

When the third daughter of the woman Wang T'ung
had shacked up with was giving birth to their third son, the
Ma-wu-k'u suddenly surged. Wailing rain had been pouring
day after day, chaperoning the arrival of Grandpa-Papa's
third grandchild-child and, at the same time, delivering long-
unseen treasures to villagers living by the rivermouth. Sand
and stone, mud and filth, scoured down from Mount Tu-K'ai,
meandered in countless watercourses through the coastal
hills, mingled with, among other things, the litter, junk and
excrement of hillbillies and their domestic animals. One by
one, the watercourses converged with the Ma-wu-k'u, which
kept gushing, stop after stop, through the mountain villages
of Mei-lan, Shang-teh, Pei-yuen-T'ai-yuen until, right after
rounding a sharp bend in the gorge, it finally reached Tung-ho
Village, on the sea. The famous soaring snowy-grey marble
arches that supported the Tung-ho Bridge, long adorned with
branches and needles, were now drowning in the clamorous
muddy waters that were desperate to hurl themselves into the
embrace of the Pacific.

Rain pitter-pattered on the sheet-iron roof. Inside, Chang
Mei-chu lay with her eyes gently shut and beads of sweat on
the lids, listening to the roaring waters of the Ma-wu-k'u and
imagining what manner of flotsam the Ma-wu-k'u would
have brought this time around. "Another transparent red
lady's slipper would be nice," she thought. "To pair with the
one I found last time." She couldn't wait to be the early-bird,
to go treasure hunting as soon as the floodwaters receded, no
matter that the red-faced baby boy curled up by her side was
still unnamed.

Mei-chu lay on a bed of four tatami mats, her big cotton quilt a patchwork of orangeish-red and white that bore a heavy musty reek from many days of torrential rain. Just as she was about to drift off, the smell of roasted yam drifted in, growing thicker and thicker as it cooked in time's oven. In the kitchen, two crewcut boys, one about six or seven and the other three or four, squatted in front of a smoking kiln, stirring every few minutes, their faces coated with soot and dirt.

Opposite the kitchen, between two bedchambers, there was a front room of less than three *p'ing*, about twenty-eight square metres. There, Grandpa-Papa Wang T'ung wasn't watching Peking Opera on the television, as he usually did at this time of the week, because of the power outage caused by the typhoon. He sat silently on his rattan chair, the mood in the room as gloomy as his face. It was two or three in the afternoon, but the dim sky made it look like it was six or seven. Grandpa-Papa turned on the pocket radio he had been using for more than a decade, which promptly broadcast the latest news of the typhoon:

Severe Typhoon Sarah is heading East North-East, and the eye of the storm has now reached 22 degrees North 122 degrees East. She is forecast to…

"Wang T'ung! You old fiend." A shrieking howl from Mei-chu's chamber. "Don't you know I'm trying to get some rest in here? Turn that damn thing off!"

He turned off the radio, without a peep. The room fell quiet again, except for the giggling of the two boys. In the dim light, his wrinkles crisscrossed the contours of his sunken cheeks, making his long skinny face look all the grimmer, like cracked clay.

A few years ago it would have been different. He would have stomped in and punched her a few times, or at least spat fuckin' cunt or bitch at her. Now, he felt old.

The first time he had felt old was two years ago in autumn.

Chang Mei-chu had just turned twenty. A voluptuous womanly glamour that other girls just did not have fairly glowed from her eyes and from her skin. When she walked on the bridge, the moaning wind blowing from the hills above the Ma-wu-k'u wrapped her clothes tightly around her figure, revealing her curves, especially her big tits, which jiggled with every step she took. Wang T'ung wasn't the only one seduced; the passersby on the bridge couldn't help noticing, either. Once parched, her skin was now moist and full. Like a shrewd young matron, emboldened by her remarkable physical appearance, she started speaking her mind, her tongue growing sharper by the day.

Over time, Wang T'ung's savage red ferocity had paled in the onslaught of Mei-chu's sarcasm. But she was still like a drippingly delicious red apple, tempting him. It was as if she could declare war at any time, issuing her challenge. One day at noon, while all the other kids were playing at their neighbours' houses, Mei-chu came back soaking wet from the rivermouth after fishing for fingerlings, her clothes revealing her curves. When Wang T'ung peeked at her from the kitchen while she was changing, his heart started pumping burning hot blood through his veins. Like a young lad, he pushed himself against Mei-chu, started to tear off her wet clothes and suck voraciously at her majestic breasts. When he was about to unbelt her trousers, she humphed sneeringly: "Let's see how long you can keep this up, you dirty old geezer!"

Wang T'ung felt dejected, like a defeated cockerel, especially when he noticed himself panting, a reminder of how feeble he was. Mei-chu turned and walked towards the bathroom, laughing nastily. No surprise that the word "old" should come to mind.

He was enraptured by Mei-chu's young spirit but at the

same time hated her youthful energy. At first Wang T'ung forbade Mei-chu from hanging out on the bridge with her pack of androgynous friends who wore their hair long and their jeans ripped. A couple of years before, when Mei-chu was only eighteen, he would just grab her and drag her home, slapping her around in front of the other kids. But now he didn't even dare walk near the youngsters, because she would just point at him while taking a drag on someone's cigarette and shout: "Hey, look who's here! That old geezer who couldn't even screw me last time he tried!"

As a matter of fact, Wang T'ung had always considered Mei-chu the most obedient of the three sisters, Mei-hua, Mei-feng and Mei-chu—*mei* for plum, the national flower, *hua* for blossom, *feng* for phoenix and *chu* for pearl. When Mei-chu's mother had brought those three daughters of hers to come shack up with him, Mei-chu was only seven. She was supposed to be in the first grade of elementary school. She had a chubby face and big round eyes, so young and adorable. She didn't look as clever as her two elder sisters, who Wang T'ung thought would turn out to be as slatternly as their mother, A-hsiang.

Over ten years ago, Wang T'ung had opened a grocery store in Chang-pin, a fishing town to the north. A-hsiang, a robust hillbilly woman with a husband at sea, used to drop in to buy booze on credit, always on her tab. Wang T'ung, who had long heard A-hsiang was a desperately sensual lady whose husband never came home, wondered how a woman like that could stand the lonely nights. She was a hard-drinker who sang and danced every time she hit the bottle. When she was high, she'd pull her dress up and mumble mumbo jumbo in her tribal tongue Amis, which Wang T'ung didn't understand a single word of.

A-hsiang and Wang T'ung hooked up because she had no money for booze. She hiked her dress up and asked him: "In exchange for some of that fine rice wine of yours?" When

Wang T'ung responded in kind, A-hsiang started crying hysterically and said: "You heartless prick! How're me and the girls supposed to live without the money you're supposed to send?" Wang T'ung's jacket was soon wet with her tears.

It was a decade already since Wang T'ung had moved to Tung-ho. He'd closed his pathetic grocery store. (Apparently business was bad because of his personality, because he was, as the neighbours said, a weirdo, offputting and unsociable, not to mention that his merchandise was always more expensive than the other shops by a dollar or two.) Wang T'ung settled down near the Tung-ho Bridge and hung up a signboard: "Wang T'ung Bonesetting." That was the first anyone had ever heard about Wang T'ung setting bones.

Wang T'ung had lived near Tung-ho Bridge for a few years before A-hsiang showed up and threw herself on his mercy. Abandoned by her old man for good, she stood by the sign holding the hands of her three little girls, who kept glancing nervously around. She stared at him with bloodshot eyes and asked him in her heavily accented Mandarin Chinese: "Let us stay wit' ya or I'm gone jump the Tung-ho Bridge and die right in front of ya. A man yer age really should have a lady around to cook and clean fer 'im."

"It's nice to fool around with A-hsiang, but what a fool I'd be if I agreed to support her and her three brats!" thought T'ung. "A-hsiang! Come to your senses! I'm a retired soldier surviving on a meagre pension, which I draw twice a year. I can't afford to feed you and your three daughters," he said.

At this, A-hsiang's eyes welled up with tears and her nose started to run. "We not gonna eat yer penshun. We's capable of catching fry and making tofu to sell. Yes, that's it! We gonna make tofu and sell it. We ain't no freeloader. Oh and... and no more drinking for me. I gonna work hard. I can work with my hand. See how strong I am!" bragged A-hsiang, straightening her back. At that, T'ung agreed to let A-hsiang stay, on condition she make a living for herself. Finally, A-hsiang had a temporary roof over her head.

That night, with her three daughters lying next to her on the tatami, A-hsiang gave Wang T'ung the hot and spicy reward that he was longing for. Wang T'ung seemed never to be satisfied. All night long, he screwed A-hsiang like he was slaughtering the communist spies long ago on the mainland, snarling the whole time, with his yellowed snaggleteeth bared and brows eyes mouth nose all crumpled up. Only then did A-hsiang and her three daughters officially become members of the Wang T'ung household.

*

The eldest sister, Mei-hua, dropped out of school when Mei-chu was in first grade. That year Mei-hua was supposed to go into sixth grade, but was sent to Taipei to work in a textile mill instead for the tidy sum of thirty thousand dollars. The day Mei-hua left, the tiny living room was crowded with the men in polyester suits who'd come to pick her up. They were chewing betel nut, their mouths and teeth stained red. Outside the door, the neighbours had gathered to see what all the fuss was about and comment on Mei-hua's appearance and demeanour. Wearing a brand new fuchsia floral print dress and a pair of black leather shoes with round plastic soles, she was cheerfully running in and out of the door, playing with her two little sisters.

"Taipei'll be so big! I'll send money home as soon as I earn some. Hey, what do you two want?" said Mei-hua. She was much taller than Mei-feng and Mei-chu, yet this was the very first time she had regarded herself as a responsible big sister. She seemed to have suddenly grown up, no longer the girl that would fight with a little sister for wearing her slippers. Mei-hua raised her chin, showing her dark skin. Her thick black watermelon rind hair swayed as she gesticulated, prouder of herself than ever.

"You won't have to do your homework now. I want to go to Taipei, too!" claimed Mei-feng. Little did she know that one day, several years later, just like her elder sister, she would regret dropping out of elementary school.

Two stripes of thick snot ran from Mei-chu's nostrils. "Can you buy a doll for me? The kind that opens and closes its eyes. I want to dress it and comb its hair," Mei-chu pleaded.

The three sisters had never got along so well as at this moment, all hopeful for the future. Chang Mei-hua kept describing how the train which she was about to take on her journey would look, and shared her idea of how prosperous Taipei would be with the curious neighbours.

"Have you ever been to Taipei?" Mei-feng asked defiantly. Her hair put into a short ponytail, Mei-feng always liked to play Miss Contrary.

"No. But that's what I often hear from the uncles inside," the eldest, Mei-hua, said smugly, despite the fact that she had just met the guests in the living room for the first time.

As everyone was so busy talking one after another, sharing impressions of Taipei, no one noticed A-hsiang sitting on the stool in the corner crying in the dark, hair dishevelled. Standing beside her, Wang T'ung was flicking through a thick stack of a hundred dollar bills with spittle on his right index finger, his big fishmouth hanging slightly open, showing his snaggleteeth, with his forehead wrinkling to the rhythm of the bill counting. After checking the amount several times, he roared impatiently at A-hsiang: "You stupid cunt! Quit your fucking whingeing! You'd think your brat was going to Taipei to sell her snatch! Quit your fussing! It's ridiculous!"

No more did Mei-chu scamper to school with her sisters as she so fondly remembered. She wore hand-me-downs, things Mei-hua left behind: a faded knee-length black skirt, a light yellow hat with brown mould stains and a hole on the right side, and a crumpled red bookbag, which, according to Mei-hua, had never been washed since it was bought. After years of exposure to the elements, it would reek with mould from time to time.

Every day, Chang Mei-chu walked all the way to the elementary school with Mei-feng. The school was located right in the middle of the village, which was roughly divided north–south. Inside the gate was a roundabout, in the centre of which stood a huge stone trapezoid, the base for a bronze statue of Sun Yat-sen, the Founding Father of the Republic of China. On either side of the roundabout stood a row of banyan trees, from the branches of which swings and trapezes were hung, and beneath which beams and seesaws were set out. To either side of the school gate stood a school patrol in a plastic yellow hat, wearing a yellow armband. "They're here to check whether students arrive on time and bow to the Founding Father," Mei-feng told Mei-chu. The first time Mei-chu went through the gate, she followed Mei-feng's lead with wholehearted sincerity, trying to be a model pupil and future citizen. Mei-chu was never remiss in her salute to the Founding Father, which she always performed with careful solemnity. No matter how many times she went in and out a day, she always bowed with the greatest respect.

It was the only thing she got right in elementary school, in retrospect, the only thing she could be proud to tell her sons about when they went to the same school. Actually, it was the only thing she could tell her kids about her school career.

*

When Mei-chu was in first grade, her form teacher, Lin Hsueh-chen, had decided she was an incurable silly goose.

"Chang Mei-chu, you stupid pig! I knew you were stupid, but is this really the best you can manage?" said Lin as she rapped the blackboard with a rattan stick, thwacking out clouds of chalk dust that fell upon Mei-chu, who, standing there at the front, could not make any headway on the maths problem.

"How many times have I told you? It's called homework because you're supposed to do it at home! Why do you never listen? Or do you like being caned?" Or "Chang Mei-chu! Do you understand what I am saying or not?" Just twenty-one, a recent graduate from the normal school, Lin Hsueh-chen was so furious the veins in her forehead stood out. Mei-chu's maths workbook whizzed from Lin's hands, like dozens of pallid leaves lying wilted on the ground.

Lin Hsueh-chen headed for the office in a rage, leaving all Mei-chu's classmates chattering wildly. Mei-chu, who didn't think it was that big a deal, knelt down slowly to pick up her exercise book. Through her fringe, however, she noticed all their gazes aimed right at her, like a pack of razor blades. She went back to her seat and tried to lower her eyes and her chin. But she could not stop her right middle finger from rolling the sweet-scented Little Angel pencil with the broken lead she had found on her way home. She had even had a quarrel with her sister Mei-feng over its ownership.

"I saw it first!"

"You liar! It was me. It was ME!"

"But it was me that picked it up first."

The two sisters had almost come to blows. The pencil ended up lying serenely in Mei-chu's stained yellow plastic pencil case. The faint fragrance of makeup powder filled the case, making the three normal pencils aromatic too. The pencils were of different lengths, two of them as long as her little finger. The unusual pencil made her feel less inferior to her classmates. But it certainly didn't help her make miracles in her workbook. She still never finished homework on time. Every day she would be punished with a caning before class was dismissed. After school, she had to stay in the empty classroom to finish her homework as the sun set. Coming home late had turned into a habit.

During break, Liu Kuo-fu, a scrawny boy who shared a desk

with her, walked past the staff room on his way to the toilet and saw Lin Hsueh-chen sitting beside the window, covering her face with a pink handkerchief and crying to another teacher, Ms Hung: "I really don't know how to teach her. She's so stupid she can't even count!" Liu Kuo-fu was so shocked he went straight back to the classroom without peeing and yelled: "Chang Mei-chu, you're in trouble! You made the teacher cry. The teacher doesn't want to teach us anymore!" As he said this, he was waving his arms frantically.

That was the start of Mei-chu's isolation.

*

A-hsiang had become a lot more diligent after moving into Wang T'ung's house. Before the sun rose, she went out to catch fish with her eldes daughtert. It took at least an hour to walk to the mouth of the Ma-wu-k'u. A-hsiang and Mei-hua each shouldered a pole of a home-strung fishing net and carried a bucket for fish and a calabash ladle, walking barefoot the whole way. Rain or shine. Fishing had become a source of money for the four women in A-hsiang's family. Sometimes, when there were a lot of fish, the four would all go to the sea, carrying four lunchboxes with dried radish, steamed peanuts and salted egg, and work the whole day. Sometimes A-hsiang would take her daughters into the mountains to gather some edible plants and make siraw (a kind of cured meat the tribal Amis often eat). A-hsiang got better and better at managing money. "One day, Kacaw will regret it." When A-hsiang crouched to gather yam leaves, she would mutter to her daughters about the mistakes their old man had made.

A-hsiang was no longer the woman who got piss-drunk every day, but when there was a feast to celebrate something in the village like the bumper harvest festival, she would still indulge. Her voice was loud and bright, her dancing beautiful. Whenever there was a celebration, people would hear her laughter and her full singing voice. She would chug bottles of rice wine until she was lying in a stupor on the floor. Mei-hua and Mei-feng were also happy to drink and chat with the neighbours, singing and dancing just like their mother, while Mei-chu would sit giggling in a corner with her mouth hanging open.

Which is why Mei-chu would end up escorting her elders home. When they got home, they would get a verbal thrashing from Wang T'ung.

"Dammit, you smelly cunts are back after getting screwed by some mutt. Hmph, you still know to come home, huh? You treat my house like a hotel and freeload off me. What do you take me for? All you know is drink, drink, drink. Your daughters are just as lousy as you, just a buncha lazy bitches."

Wang T'ung's hands were behind his back and his grey, blue-veined head kept nodding non-stop. Through the gaps between his snaggleteeth, rancid spittle spouted, landing in the dense hair of the four females in front of him. The thick, slimy liquid clung feebly to the curly pitch of darkness of A-hsiang's hair, struggling and squirming. A-hsiang used her Mandarin, which was now quite fluent, to refute him.

"Old Wang, be honest, in all these days, have I ever took a single cent from ya? I cook the meals, wash the clothes, and serve you in every single way. Buying a wife would cost you at least a hundred thousand dollars. If you think I'm selling my cunt, then pay up next time you do it! Dammit, you can thank your lucky stars I got matched with you, you old Chinaman. What do you have to complain about?"

"You ungrateful stinky snatch, if I don't teach you a lesson, you're never gonna know your place. See if I don't beat you to dea—" said Wang T'ung until A-hsiang threw up rancid vomit all over his blueish-grey jacket. Slimy bits flowed down Wang T'ung's arm and dripped onto his bony yet surprisingly gigantic fingers. He slapped A-hsiang across her filthy face.

After all the scolding and beating, when Wang T'ung had

his needs in the night, he would turn over and pounce on A-hsiang. Asleep or awake, he would drop his drawers and penetrate her vigorously. The strength he mustered was like resentment pent up for hundreds of thousands of years, or like a will to overcome in mortal combat, each thrust increasingly forceful, his prowess seemingly inexhaustible. Nobody would have thought that the swift thrusts in the darkness were by a fifty-year-old, whose body under the shine of a fluorescent light was dry, saggy, covered in a web of wrinkles.

In the darkness, Mei-chu would blink her big eyes and peer in the direction of the sucking noises to see, to her amazement, her mother pressed under Wang T'ung's body. As the thrusts got faster and faster, she would search out her mother's gaze, but her mother never opened her eyes, only occasionally muttered: "Old Wang, can you get it over with already, I've got to go fishing tomorrow morning." Mei-chu, believing her mother was awake, sought a sense of safety in the darkness, but couldn't tell where her mama's voice was coming from, left, right, front or back. The disappearance of any sense of safety left her waking up to the same sound each night, watching Wang T'ung withdraw from her mother's groin and turning over her own, small body, only pretending to be asleep, only willing to close her eyes and drift off when she held her mother's thick, pliant body. Her fear of the dark hadn't changed when she turned twenty-one, as she still worried that if she but closed her eyes everything would change shape and assault her ravenously, or that the world would have disappeared when she opened her eyes, leaving her all alone.

One time when she woke in the middle of the night she discovered that Wang T'ung did the exact same thing to her elder sister Mei-feng. She hid under the blanket, searching for her sister's gaze with one eye, but her sister's whole body was crushed under Wang T'ung's weight. Not seeing anything, she went groggily back to sleep. When Wang T'ung did the same to her, she was ready, knowing it was inevitable. She didn't think there was anything strange about it.

*

When she was in third grade, two big things happened. The first was that after moving the classroom to the only upper floor in the school, Ms Lin, now Mrs Lin, announced to the whole class that she wouldn't hit the students anymore. This was good news to Chang Mei-chu, undoubtedly. But it didn't mean she could avoid a daily beating, because Mrs Lin delegated the task to the model student Fenny Chuang. And the first to be experimented on was Mei-chu, who could never finish her homework on time.

According to the one-line-two-sticks rule, Chang Mei-chu would get fourteen stripes on her palms. When the stick in Fenny's hand fell feebly on Mei-chu's plump fingers, she didn't withdraw her hands as swiftly as usual. The kids seemed to have predicted this display. Beams of sunlight wove into layers as laughter echoed. Mrs Lin straightened up abruptly, standing in front of the first row of desks, her massive form blocking the languid golden sunshine from sprinkling into the first class of the morning. "Harder, Fenny," she said. "Or you'll be next."

When the rattan was upraised, in the moment before it came whipping down, Mei-chu got a clear glimpse of apology in Fenny's eyes. After the beating started, one of Fenny's little hands wielded the whip while the other desperately clutched at the blue dress with shoulder straps, the corners of her lips clenching towards her cheeks to the rhythm of the whips. Compared to Fenny's downcast face, Chang Mei-chu felt her slouch, incredibly, straighten up, for the first time in Mrs Lin's class. The atmosphere in the room turned grave, the whoosh of the cane appearing out of some remote nameless land. Birds chirped in her ears. Boats on the Pacific Ocean were close at hand, and sunshine glittered on the ripples. Even the creepy, cratered visage of Witch Hill behind the school softened its gaze. Mei-chu didn't feel the pain at all. She even started grinning despite herself.

"You got to fight to know someone," as the soap opera *Bodyguard* put it. It seemed to fit her relationship with Fenny. Before then, she had never thought of giving Fenny unripe green mangos (which Wang T'ung had warned her repeatedly not to pick) and *siraw*. She sun-dried the meat on a plate and wrapped it carefully with pages torn from an exercise book, putting it carefully in her bag, unaware of the odour. When she laid that *siraw* on Fenny's desk, her halting stutter took Fenny, now wearing her hair in plaits, aback.

"Th-this is *siraw*, it's for you. M-m-my mum made it."

When she saw Fenny put the meat into the drawer, she decided to bring some mangos the following day.

But unbeknownst to her, Fenny, having accepted the *siraw*, couldn't stand the smell, and dropped it for a mangy dog to eat on her way home. But she did say she enjoyed the sour green mangos, her mouth puckering and her eyes squinting. Even at the risk of being beaten by the skinny old Wang T'ung, Mei-chu kept up their relationship, considering it the most worthwhile thing she had ever done. She didn't realize her feeling for Fenny was actually admiration, or even worship, such that even after the second major event ended their relationship she still took the heat for Fenny, without hesitation, to preserve the girl's spotless reputation. Having to shave her head due to the lice epidemic resolved Mei-chu never to cut her hair again.

"Chang Mei-chu, smells like poo, doesn't wash when she should, would give her classmates lice if she could, shame on you, Chang Mei-chu," chanted Liu Kuo-fu in class. Long before the dress and hygiene check when Mrs Lin found lice in Fenny's waist-length hair, Mei-chu had already been shocked to discover the secret in Fenny's locks. Carefully and silently, she'd picked out the tiny lice eggs for Fenny once already. It sounded surprisingly loud when Mei-chu popped them fiercely with her thumbnails. Soon she had lice in her own hair, and had to get her head shaved. The patterned kerchief on her bald head gave out a camphor-oil scent from time to time. Fenny, who'd had a close crop, like a soldier's, solemnly announced: "My mum said I can't play with you anymore."

*

Mei-chu tied her hip-length hair into a bun, but it couldn't resist the warm breeze blowing from the swaying whistling pines on the banks of the Ma-wu-k'u, strands of loose hair dancing by her ears and neck. After the flood receded, Mei-chu chose a sunny day to take her sons Ming-pao and Ming-t'ai treasure hunting. Driftwood from upstream was mixed into the rocks and sand on the riverbank, embellishing the well-washed daily essentials, things like the transparent lady's slipper Mei-chu had been hoping would appear.

Mei-chu strolled, glancing along the bank and bending down occasionally to throw items she picked up into the bamboo basket on her back. Following behind, Ming-pao and Ming-t'ai leaped around, chasing fleeing hermit crabs. From a hundred metres away Mei-chu saw two young fellows on the cobblestones at the estuary skimming rocks. The light was so bright she had to block the sun with her palm over her forehead to make out the strangers' faces. One of them, who was missing his left arm, had a strong throwing arm, the stones skipping five or six times before taking the plunge. His left sleeve swung back and forth with the force of each throw.

Mei-chu was entranced watching them until, in a moment of carelessness, she was tripped by the walking stick she was carrying. *Thump!* She flopped heavily down on the rocks. Feeling fortunate to have such a wide and plump backside, she noticed the strangers were watching her, whispering. The one-armed stranger had a flattop. His skin was tanned and glowing, framing those piercing eyes, like a shark's, though she had no idea how shark eyes looked. Certainly she did not think she would leave her hometown and go to the other side of the mountains after the harvest festival with this shark-eyed man, never in a million years.

She struggled to stand up, her ample bosom bouncing, trying to free itself from the tight cloth. The other fellow curbed his urge to whistle and tapped the shark-eyed guy's shoulder, saying: "A pair of bazookas to rival Aphrodite A," in reference to a robot anime character who could shoot rockets out of her chest. "Damn, you must really have been starved on the boat? I've seen bigger." In the evening, a bunch of androgynous young people gathered on the bridge over the Ma-wu-k'u. Some sat on bicycles, others leaned on the red cement railings.

Right after dinner, before the sun had set, the evening breeze blew slowly from the crest of Mount Tung-ho. A bus, fully loaded with passengers, crossed the bridge from the other side, swaying and shaking it. "The Ding Dong bus!" the young people screamed gleefully when the bus roared by. They waved at the passengers or spat betel nut husks and cigarette butts at the bus.

One of them, a long-haired boy with pimples and stubble on his gaunt, chiselled face, ran after the smoky black exhaust puffing out of the tail. His knees high, leaning forward, he ran after the bus, shouting: "The Ding Dong bus! The Ding Dong bus! Nobody wants to ride in the Ding Dong bus!"

That would make the youngsters double over with laughter. If the driver was in a bad mood he'd stick his head out the window and roar: "Fuck off, you rotten kids! Want to get run over?" Like a disembodied demon's head. Which only made them laugh harder, jumping up and down and yelling the same thing, louder and louder. In this pack of youngsters that hung out on the bridge, Mei-chu seemed more lively and spirited and deft, much more. Her powerfully reedy voice would break in from time to time, pure and sweet. With a few bags of peanuts to snack on and a few bottles of rice wine to wash them down, the youngsters could while away an afternoon on the bridge. The topics of conversation would change with the seasons. With the approach of summer, how many would the Ma-wu-k'u grab to die in others' stead? How many would move to and from the village? How had the Ding Dong bus run over that nice old man one stormy night? Who'd sold their daughter to build a concrete house? Who saw the long-gowned lady ghost sticking out her thin pallid tongue, hanging out under the bridge in the middle of an inky night? A few years ago, when Mei-chu got pregnant with her first son, infuriating her mother A-hsiang into leaving, the gossips had a field day. But now it was Mei-chu taking issue with how other folks were acting. People forget easily. And people get used to things when they see them often enough. It comes to seem natural. But for Mei-chu, the cyclic alternation of the seasons was marked with some fresh realizations.

Mei-chu met the shark-eyed man at the harvest festival. After the seven-day event ended, she left home with him and went to Taipei, a place she'd only dreamed of. She knew the day would come, and had dreamed of such a man appearing in her life. The shark-eyed man had only to ask: "Would you like to come with me?" Seeing her chance, Mei-chu started nodding. "I'll get my things together tonight. We'll leave tomorrow morning, all right?" Then like A-hsiang, she gave the shark-eyed man a spicy, hot reward, on the grass beside the yam field behind the elementary school.

Pressed under the man on the grass, Mei-chu heard the bell bracelets around her wrists and ankles tinkling. On her legs, leggings, and many skirts around her waist. The shark-eyed man's one arm, his right, was nimble. He scratched his head, annoyed, and said: "These tribal clothes and decorations you're wearing are really a lot of trouble."

Chang Mei-chu cackled. "Don't take anything off! I still

have a show to do," she said, tinkling her bells theatrically. Her eyes half open, she saw a black kite circling for ages over Witch Hill. She wasn't sure if it was the same one she saw in elementary school. The first time she saw it was the day she got her period in fifth grade. That day, blood flowed all over her chair in the middle of class. She didn't feel any pain, just sat there in a cold sweat, having no idea what to do, but the boy who sat next to her, Liu Kuo-fu, saw, raised his hand, and said: "Chang Mei-chu's bleeding."

The teacher gave her a pile of tissues and told her to go to the toilet. After helping her pack her bookbag, her teacher asked her to go home to see her mum.

On the way back home, she felt like she'd bled out all her blood. She felt weak, like she was about to die. Looking up, she saw the dark shadow of a black kite circling. Her heart beat faster, her sight blurred, she was nearly petrified with fear. She couldn't help thinking of the story she had once heard:

A cruel black kite lives on Witch Hill. When it's hungry, it will beat its huge wings, soar into the sky and circle for food. Once it notices a child alone, it will dive down and seize it.

Chang Mei-chu pressed her mouldy yellow student cap low and walked with great difficulty, for her legs felt like jelly. Peeping at the big bird from under the brim, she was afraid that it sensed the smell of blood and would prey on her. After she finally made it home, she let herself cry out at the front door to the house: "Come out, Mum! I'm dying. My bottom's bleeding."

Her mum wasn't at home, but her cries drew Wang T'ung out.

"Come here. Let me take a look." She was told to take off her trousers to see if she was sick. In a few seconds, Wang T'ung pushed her to the wicker chair in the living room and put his body over hers. The lower part of her body hurt her so much she screamed, as if she had been torn to pieces. She had a vague memory of her shaking head pressed down by his big, coarse hands, his gruff voice repeating:

"Oh titties! You are very sick, little girl."

*

Chang Mei-chu gasped for air, her whole body burning, overwhelmed by the thrill just now. The shark-eyed man withdrew his body from hers, still dazed by the softness of her generous breasts. Mei-chu's body, clammy and sticky, started to itch all over from the tingling of the grassy ground. She caught a glimpse of the hawk still circling in the sky and could not help but burst out laughing, her whole body trembling. "It's spying on us," Mei-chu said, still in the shark-eyed man's embrace, soothing her itches by scratching them. Soon after, both of them started giggling again.

The imminent arrival of the harvest festival brought excitement and work for Mei-chu, who was so busy every day preparing the song-and-dance numbers that she didn't immediately notice the changes that had come over Wang T'ung.

Wang T'ung got accustomed to moving that rattan chair to the entrance and sitting there several hours at a time. His pipe puffing away, nothing caught his attention, not even the cars going past. It went on like this for several months. During the night, when Wang T'ung could not fall asleep, he put on a jacket over his pyjamas and walked to the Tung-ho Bridge.

The bridge seemed even more peaceful at night. Wang T'ung would generally put both his hands behind his back and pace back and forth across the bridge, his flip-flops squeaking. Intermittently, in syncopation with his steps, the crashing noise of the ocean waves or, sometimes, the howling of a stray dog could be heard.

The old-fashioned street lamps of the bridge illuminated his face, making him look particularly gloomy and wretched, like he was about to collapse. The light, however, did not reach his lower body, giving the impression that he was floating in the darkness, like a peripatetic lost soul. Soon, a rumour rustled through the village.

"The floating ghost on the bridge is a man, not a woman."

The less communicative Wang T'ung was, the more conspicuous Mei-chu's sharp intelligence became. Soon after Mei-chu gave birth to her third child, Wang T'ung was told to go and sleep in the room used to pile up all the junk. After that, they would avoid each other even during meals. Frequently, contrary to Wang T'ung's expectations, the children would call for their father to come and have a bowl of rice with them. They would call for a long time. However, as soon as dinner was ready, Wang T'ung would turn on the radio and wait until Mei-chu and the children had taken their fill before eating the leftovers, facing away from the table.

Wang T'ung would get harangued by Mei-chu at the drop of a hat for his faults, driven into a corner. Sometimes, scolded harshly and spitefully, he would take refuge in his room and pack his peeling wooden suitcase, as if he was all ready to go at any time. He'd hiss at his sons: "Daddy's taking you back to our hometown in China, we're not staying here and letting the bitch wear us down." To Mei-chu, his fantasies of going home were evidence of insanity. She did not take any notice of him.

After New Year, Daddy Wang, the infamous pockmark-faced fellow who lived on Mount Tung-ho, went back to his hometown in China for a family visit, returning with a letter for Wang T'ung from his middle-aged nephew. No more than a messenger, Daddy Wang did not even bother to greet Wang T'ung face-to-face. He only left a few words for Mei-chu to pass on: "Tell him to go back and see what things are like!"

Ever since Wang T'ung had got news from home, his mind had come unhinged. The other day Mei-chu even heard him in his tiny bedroom weeping, his voice hoarse and low, as unpleasant as a knife scratching glass, grating on Mei-chu's ears. As she was searching for the source of the noise, she murmured: "This is giving me the goosebumps!" Upon realizing that Wang T'ung's bedroom was locked, she turned down the corridor and peeked through the window to see him squatting on his plank bed, looking as if his soul had left him. In a confluence of spittle, snot and tears. At the sight, Mei-chu couldn't help but rage: "I guess you can't wait to meet your maker, huh? In the middle of the day, crying a body to the grave! What's there to cry about? Crazy!"

Wang T'ung burst into tears again the day Mei-chu left. But she didn't notice it, because he buried his head in the heavy cotton-padded blanket and curled himself up like a terribly wronged child. Deliberately stifling his whimpers, his shrivelled, aged body couldn't help but shake at every snivel. Mei-chu had spent the entire night packing. Before she left, she woke her two sons Ming-pao and Ming-t'ai and said: "Mummy is going to Taipei to look for work. This time I'm only taking your youngest brother. But after everything's settled, I will come back for you two. You boys have to behave yourselves. No fighting, okay?" As she was leaving, she gently patted their cheeks. "As soon as I have earned some money, I will bring you boys something. Tell me, is there anything you want?" The way she said it was exceptionally gentle. So much like Chang Mei-hua, leaving home for the big city years before. Blinking, she'd promised Mei-chu a doll. Later, she did keep her promise. But the look of the doll was less than ideal— grimy, dishevelled and wan-looking – just like Mei-hua. The overjoyed Mei-chu, holding her new toy, had no idea what had happened to her sister, whose eyes were dull and empty and whose body was terribly bruised. A few days later, the visitor with his smile red with betel nut juice showed up again. Not only did he take Mei-hua away again, but also the middle sister Mei-feng, leaving another generous stack of bills—a hundred grand—for Wang T'ung to count.

Chang Mei-chu kept her appointment with the shark-eyed man, and they took the first Ding Dong bus to town, then a northbound train. The moment Chang Mei-chu got on, she was unusually excited, smiling foolishly at her companion. She was thinking that Mei-hua had left, Mei-feng had left, Mum had left, and now so had she. Ming-pao and Ming-t'ai would also leave before long. Ruminating over this idea, she turned her head and smiled again at the man who was taking her away. He knew nothing, just thought she was happy to take a trip on a train. So he smiled back.

Two months later, when Chang Mei-chu went back to Tung-ho for Ming-pao and Ming-t'ai she was informed that Wang T'ung had drowned in the Ma-wu-k'u. When his body was fished out, blood oozed from all the holes in his head, and his body was black and swollen. Henceforth she would hear Wang T'ung wailing mutely at night, choking and hoarse. The drowned head floated and sank in the dirty yellow water, crying out in her dreams. She realized he was past sixty when he died, that the old man she yelled at through the window panes was a ghost who could not do anything else but howl. His pink and bloodless face smiling from ear to ear, showing his snaggleteeth. He was clearly smiling, but he sounded pathetic, weeping hoarsely. The ghost had ruined the four Chang women, showing up for no reason and disappearing for no reason. If Chang Mei-chu hadn't had three sons, who were alive and kicking right in front of her, she would have thought it was a nightmare that lasted twenty years, that Wang T'ung was only a ghost. A ghost from the other side of the Taiwan Strait who spoke a different language, a ghost with a mysterious and unimaginable past.

Whenever Chang Mei-chu was awakened by the sound of the splashing of the Ma-wu-k'u, she heard, as if in a trance, Wang T'ung's drowning head screaming for help. Chang Mei-chu tried to escape, but she was always swept away in the nightmare by the sky-high waves of the Ma-wu-k'u. She opened her eyes and sobbed: "There's no escape, no escape."

No, Chang Mei-chu could not escape. The Ma-wu-k'u is still flushing down, carrying rubbish, castaways and faeces discharged by the people upstream and their pigs and chickens living upstream. Everything flowed into that Ma-wu-k'u. The scenery along the river didn't change. Stories about veterans and tribal women made the rounds from time to time, just like before. But the thing she couldn't shake was the nightmare of the Ma-wu-k'u, which oozed everywhere the water went, lingering on with its last breath.

The Last Whistling Pine, Forgotten by the Windbreak

1. **Was A-ma crazy?**

I HADN'T NOTICED ANYTHING ODD BEFORE A-MA OF THE Dragon clan came over for the third time to ask when my little brother A-chung would be back. Busybody Chang was squatting by the pool, vigorously ladling water onto a big fat chicken, whose puckered skin, freshly plucked and scalded, was steaming. He snatched some feathers from the steel basin, hurled them into the ditch, and bawled: "That half-breed, nothing but a troublemaker!"

I knew it was perfect timing for me to ask: "What happened?"

My keen-eyed mother, who happened to be coming out of the kitchen with a bundle of mustard greens, gave me that look.

"Enough questions." My lips were immediately zipped. "Spoiled brat," she kept grumbling. "His mother's fault. If Big Daddy Dragon were still around, things wouldn't have got so out of hand."

Just a dozen minutes passed before A-ma swung by for the fourth time. With big dark circles under his eyes, he looked woozy, his flabby belly wobbling as he lurched around.

"Is A-chung back yet?" he said, his voice evincing extreme disquiet. My dad, with his accustomed light step, so light he seemed to be a practitioner of the kung fu of lightness, came over to find out what was up. "Uncle, I'm dead mea..." A-ma said despairingly. Then, like a somnambulist, he dragged himself out of our hundred-metre yard. My dad must have been in on a big secret, stuffed with nightmarish fantasies and unfolding like the autumnal swaying of the whistling pine trees arrayed around our property, excluding me like I was an outsider. I was after all the child who'd left home a long time ago to pursue my education in the big city in the north. My returns would often bring a slight commotion to the village, disrupting its stasis.

I should mention here that I was the first college student worthy of the name in the village. You might with your city standards not think much of the achievement, but the day the list of which students had been accepted to which university was put up on the bulletin board, the villagers set off firecrackers they'd been storing up for months, as if confirming the prophecy made by Big Daddy Dragon many years before, shaking heaven and earth deep into the night. For this reason, every time I come back, I have to make my rounds of the uncles of the village, paying my respects by bowing and letting them rub my little cold hands in their big callused palms, which patted my loose Michelle Pfeiffer curls and pinched my fat cheeks. They would natter on about all the important things that had been going on in the village. The speed of death spread like an epidemic among the uncles, faster than the needles of the whistling pine trees floated down to the ground. Immersed in the shadows of the withering and dying of their comrades, my uncles, a.k.a. the Old Stags—the ageing veterans of the War of Resistance Against Japan and the Chinese Civil War—would prick my hands with palms so callused I thought of porcupines as they told me, drunk on dreams, of the bizarre visions their brothers-in-arms had brought them from the land of the dead. But this time they seemed on guard, as if I were an outsider, an invader. Which depressed me.

At the cost of washing the dinner dishes and buying a bunch of firecrackers, and with the aid of some things I heard from my naughty little sister, a foolish and greedy girl, and my fat little brother. "A-ma, he's crazy," my sister said. "Pa-ra-noid. Goes around saying someone's trying to kill 'im!"

"Oh, right, don't forget to let me check after you finish with the dishes," my fat kid brother said. "A-ma, he went and sold his girlfriend." With a swoosh, a firecracker flew by my skirt into the heavens above the yard, a red flower blooming over the tips of the branches of a whistling pine tree.

The autumn arrived at Mimi's and my hometown, its manner exceedingly slow and hesitant. First, you heard the hoarse soughing of the whistling pines, like the voice of a deaf man, like the dialect of the old veterans when they started babbling, their speech degenerating in anticipation of death. Then you saw the thin branches of the whistling pines dancing gracefully in the breeze, like an Amis girl's instinctive talent originated in ancient, obscure myth.

It was that same autumn, a year ago, that I walked into the trap Mimi had set. And this past spring, when my creative writing professor was pressuring me to hand in my draft, Mimi spoke. "You are me," she said. Though I was baffled and tried every way I could to refute her, I couldn't help realizing different prophetic possibilities, step by step.

The ritual of worship of all the ancestors in the tree on a mid-autumn night has been a long-standing practice in my family for thousands of years. But this year for the first time, we were even worshipping folks to whom we have no blood relation. I wondered whether my aunts and uncles living in another charmed realm of rivers and mountains, with whom we'd lost touch since China and Taiwan were separated in 1949, would practise our family ritual and worship my father and third uncle, who had left their hometown long ago when they were young.

The ritual always begins with a dinner symbolic of reunion, for which the preparations are laborious. In the early morning, the old bachelors gather near the cistern in our yard, sharpening blades to butcher chickens and ducks. Even earlier, you might notice them selecting a fat sheep from Big Daddy Dragon's stall or catching a big carp in the fishpond. Or you might hear Marathon turning his mill, grinding peas. But every year there are fewer uncles working and more uncles to worship. That was why Busybody Chang was working alone this Mid-Autumn Festival, looking sullen.

The eldest son in our family, A-chung, was home before the ritual started. As spirit money burnt fiercely in the drum and sparkled up into the air above the yard, A-chung knelt, with his back towards the front door, kowtowed three times, and held a stick of incense as he followed Mother, muttering. On the big round table facing the door, ritual dishes were set out, along with small cups of wine and a little rice in about a dozen bowls, around a big glass bowl of rice in which an upright stick of incense smouldered. Ma said that our ancestors would eat for as long as the smoke of the incense rose, and only then could we, the descendants, enjoy the meal.

Still wearing her hair in a ponytail, Mimi stepped on a round stool to climb up onto the table and sneak a piece of cold sliced chicken. Fleet-footed Father appeared out of nowhere and slapped her on her burning cheek. "You mustn't insult the ancestors," Father, who had always been good-tempered, roared in a panic.

"But I didn't see any ancestor, not even one."

"Are you talking back?"

But Mimi told me that this time she really did see the ancestors, and the Old Stags. Big Daddy Dragon came, too, complaining his son was unfilial, his wife untrue, so he had nowhere to go at Mid-Autumn, which is why he showed up here at our place. As it happened, A-ma Dragon showed up once again, for the fifth time. Except for Mimi, nobody noticed him hiding in a corner in the backyard, half-covering his face.

The milky moonlight swayed with the sparse branches, casting shifting shadows on his face, sometimes cyan and sometimes white. Mimi said it was scary. A-ma hissed across the window screen. "A-chung, A-chung. Come out!" But instead of A-chung out came Big Daddy Dragon. "You're a rotten sheep. I'm gone only a few years and my son is a wastrel, my wife an adulteress who dissipated the family fortune and slept around. Don't think I won't teach you a lesson just because your mother protects you. I'll give you such a beating you'll never forget."

A-ma grabbed the wooden frame of our window screen, knocking his head on it and shaking it. "Forgive me, please, forgive me…" My little brother A-chung dragged A-ma in and gave him a bowl of hot liqueur with an egg. At the sight of my brother in his starched police uniform, A-ma quickly gathered his wits.

"A-chung, somebody's trying to kill me," he said, sucking the drool from the corners of his mouth.

"I know, I've only heard you say so, what, a hundred times."

"But you don't believe me."

"If I didn't believe you, would I help you find a hiding place?"

You have no idea what special authority the police uniform my brother had just put on symbolized. Keeping his breathing even, A-chung told my unruly kid sister and fat little brother not to butt in and to go and take care of the dishes and chopsticks. Then he began questioning A-ma calmly. "A-ma, I want you to be honest with me. Do you have any idea where Uya is?"

My little sister, stacking the oily bowls and plates on the table for washing, said: "A-ma, he's crazy." Carrying the bowls and plates to the sink, my fat little brother made a face at A-ma and said: "A-ma, he went and sold his woman." My mum picked up a feather duster and gave them both a smack on the backside. "How many times do I have to tell you two, no rumour mongering!" A-ma's woman's name was Uya. Where had she got to? Mimi said that she had hidden herself in the moon, playing the part of Lady Ch'ang-o, the woman in the moon in Chinese myth. That explained why the moon was so round and so bright this Mid-Autumn Festival.

2. In search of A-ma's missing fiancée

A-MA'S FIANCÉE, UYA, WAS AN AMIS ABORIGINAL GIRL. Skinny and sickly, she appeared like a shadow without history, moving into A-ma's house in a blink. "My son A-ma's getting married. Oh! Great! His wife's gonna look after him. He ain't gonna get into trouble no more," A-ma's mother, Ruby, cheerfully declared to everyone she met, regardless of the fact she'd said the exact same thing eight years ago when A-ma was sixteen years old. A-ma's fiancée back then was an Amis girl as well. Back then Big Daddy Dragon wasn't so cheerful. In fact the thunder of his rage swept the whole village. "A-ma's gotta enroll in military academy and become an officer and recover the homeland we lost!" he roared, inadvertently spreading the news about A-ma getting married far and wide. From then on, every now and then, villagers would deliberately walk by the fishpond by A-ma's house, peek in across the small concrete bridge, and yell: "Hey, A-ma, when ya getting married?" "After I go to Taipei and earn my fortune!" A-ma would reply from inside the house, if he was in the mood.

But few had got a look at A-ma's fiancée. Pappy Shou, who had long ears, a symbol of good fortune, declared, "She is as tame as a baby goat. She does what you tell her to, a very obedient young lady. A-ma's a lucky guy!" "A baby goat? Nah! She's more likely a cat, I say. Gloomy girl she is. She only seems to go along, truth is she's a shrew! Watch out for her claws!" Busybody Chang, who lived across the street from Pappy Shou, said with his usual disagreeable urgency. At the time,

A-ma's fiancée was three months pregnant.

A-ma's fiancée was neither a baby goat nor a cat. Instead, she was like a bunny. Mimi said: "You couldn't forget the sight of Uya following behind A-ma on the soft sandy bank of the Hsiu-ku-luan, A-ma taking big steps and Uya hopping along, trying to catch up with him. Uya was a lonely woman without a voice, yet her figure was more like a prepubescent girl's. There was always fear in her big, dewy eyes. Whenever the wind blew, meaning the grass had better bend, she would hitch up her white skirt and her skinny legs would move frantically, leaving scattered little footprints on the sand. The disarray of her prints was as pitiful as her delicate palm-sized face, which was often hidden by her soft tawny hair. Despite her pale skin and the dark half-moons under her eyes, no man would be attracted by her bony figure, as sexy as a two-by-four. She's not the kind of woman as brings good luck to her husband."

Mimi, you were still unconsciously radiating jealous hostility because of your secret teenage crush on A-ma. But A-ma was no longer the same A-ma who looked so heroic before he turned eighteen. His brain had run to fat, his eyes gone cloudy, his expression dazed, his limbs clumsy, his every movement sluggish. What was there to feel jealous about?

On lunar New Year's Day, A-ma put his two years behind the wheel of a taxi to use by driving us, and the neighbours' kids, down the coast from the Ma-wu-k'u to the Hsiu-ku-luan. That was when I met the fabled bride-to-be Uya.

She sat in the shotgun seat, beside A-ma, holding a stupid furry white dog with a red bow on its head. It was just like when I was young and my parents would lead a bunch of village ragamuffins over hill and dale to the mountaintop, for a stunning view of the Pacific. All along the way we'd sing a mixed chorus march under my father's vigorous baton: "Crush the Russian Bandits, Counter Communism (Counter Communism)! Annihilate the Bandits, Slaughter Traitors to the Han Race! (Slaughter Traitors to the Han Race!)" My father, in his classic lyric tenor voice, would teach us how to sing the "Blood-Stained Yellow Flowers", the pride of the officers trained in the Huang-p'u Military Academy. Then, in a change of mood, he'd announce a popular song such as would gratify a cabaret audience. "And next, ladies and gentlemen, I present to you: 'A Game, A Dream'." My mother would take the imaginary microphone and sing karaoke, her body swaying to the rhythm: *left, right, left, right, left, right.*

> *Who can ever really know*
> *my misery, dancing in a show?*
> *My tears about to fall,*
> *I fake a smile*
> *Ah… shall we dance?*
> *If I miss a step*
> *No matter how you seem*
> *I'll pretend we're in a dream*

This time, in A-ma's taxi, when all the people were waving hands and swaying their bodies to my mother's sharp, karaoke-style singing voice, you might have, like me, discovered Uya was a woman without a voice. She huddled in the black leather shotgun seat like the furry dog in her arms. All the people in the car began to hoot and egg the bride-to-be on to sing a song. You saw Uya's scrawny wrist on the steering wheel in A-ma's grasp pull back, slithering away like a tiny snake and hiding itself in the depths of the black leather seat. And all you heard was the stupid furry white dog whining. "This harpy's hands must be wrapped round the stupid furry dog's neck to hurt it, like a little white snake," Mimi said knowingly.

I wondered if A-ma's chick might be dumb, so she never understood my kindhearted attitude towards her, which welled up from the bottom of my heart. When I distributed the food and drink, I handed her two cokes, and seized the opportunity to introduce myself, in an I-think-I-am-funny way: "I was A-ma's playmate when he was still wearing open-crotch pants."

Uya now seemed to be a shocked hare. She squeezed behind A-ma's thick arm, trying to hide herself behind his flabby body, her hands clutching the margins of his clothes with her hawklike claws. She peered out at me through the crack between his sleeve and his torso, her eyes gleaming red.

Uya was not dumb. When A-ma talked to her in fluent Amis, she responded in short syllables with a nasally sweet voice like a little girl's. What astonished us was that A-ma had picked up the tribal tongue with such proficiency. You would have had no idea that A-ma had been stuttering since he was little, his only flaw during his heroic age, which lasted until he turned eighteen.

This was the first time that I met Uya and the last time as well. A month later, Uya went missing.

Where could a pregnant woman go? Various rumours spread fantastically between the dancing branches and the needles of the whistling pines.

1. A-ma's enemy captured Uya, denying him descendants out of maliciousness.
2. Uya, an ill-fated lady who couldn't bear the thought of the hardship or poverty she would have to endure, had absconded.
3. Uya was a playgirl and some lad she went out with before couldn't bear the blow of her engagement and had seduced her, got her to elope with him.
4. Uya came from a prominent tribal family, the elders of which had hid her with shamanic magic because either they didn't want her to break the tradition according to which the man married into the woman's family or they

couldn't accept the contamination of their bloodline with Han Chinese blood.

5. Big Daddy Dragon's ghost, disapproving of A-ma's impending marriage, let alone to a hillbilly daughter-in-law, came out to play tricks every night. Uya could not stand it so she jumped into the Pacific.

6. A-ma sold Uya to feed his drug addiction.

Rumours were still festering…

It wasn't hard to conclude from these hypotheticals that the ageing uncles would stand by A-ma no matter what the truth was but that everyone thought he was a useless son, a son who would ruin the family. A-chung, my younger brother who had just graduated from the police academy, had already started searching for information about A-ma's lost girlfriend like a keen hunting dog to prove his potential as an outstanding officer. It was then that A-ma, who had already turned into a fat pig, sensed that his heroic age had passed, that he had been replaced by A-chung, Mr Nobody. He hadn't lived up to Big Daddy Dragon's dying wish: "Reclaim your father's glorious history!" Thinking about it, he would often kneel down on the path through the grove of whistling pines and wail: "Dad, I'm back. And I'm sorry!"

Was A-ma crazy? Yes, he was, A-chung said, and he'd gone crazy before autumn came. It had been a disastrous summer: that typhoon season, three hundred and sixty-five whistling pine trees in the windbreak had been blown down, and there was another freak fire.

3. Young man A-ma's heroic spirit

YOU MIGHT NOT BELIEVE IT, BUT WHEN A-MA HAD YET TO reach the age of eighteen, he was really handsome. All the girls in the village ached to be all grown up so they could marry him. They had learned infighting and intrigue with one another since they were very young. These overt and covert struggles continued until A-ma was sixteen and pledged his love to another girl, until he became a useless butterball.

A-ma had been a good-looking baby: a sleek egg-shaped head, a prominent and broad forehead, a shiny and symmetrical face—even features, in all respects revealing his exceptionally graceful, heroic manner. Big Daddy Dragon loved feeling the round shape of his head and the fullness of his forehead. "Son, I want you to be like Him," he said, not needing to specify who "He" was. You'd notice the resemblance of young man A-ma's prompt salute to a well-trained regular soldier's and then, following Big Daddy Dragon's reverent and almost idolizing gaze, you'd see the portrait of a man in military attire, hung up high on the right side of the living room. The portrait, of which the frame was always spotlessly clean, showed a man named Chiang . (You had to leave an extra space before and after his name to avoid being accused of intent to slander the commander-in-chief of our nation.) A-ma evidently shared some similarities in appearance with the mighty leader. Which is why the Old Stags loved him, the little brats in the village feared him, and even the schoolteachers respected him.

"A-ma is gonna be a brass hat!" Everyone in the village loved patting A-ma's shiny head. "Look at that head, he's born to be a bureaucrat." A-ma wasn't a disappointment yet, in those days. As a boy, he could tell a story supposedly attesting to Chiang Kai-shek's courage and wisdom—the story of Chiang firing back at a Japanese instructor's racist analogy at the expense of the Chinese people, that four hundred million germs in a clod of dirt represented the Chinese people: Chiang broke the clod into eight and said the fifty million germs in one of the pieces represented the Japanese. He would also stand between the two fishponds Big Daddy Dragon had built for him, and look at the fish swimming up the slope against the flow, a reference to the story of salmon who took inspiration from the indomitable Chiang. A-ma really did have the best salute. We used to play a game where the winner responded the fastest with a salute to the name of the leader. A-ma always won.

A-ma had an exceptional name—Lung Chi-Ma (Dragon, Unicorn-Horse)—the story of which he never got tired of telling. "On the day I was born, my dad dreamed of a dragon jumping out of a cloud and onto a beautiful white horse. The horse ran fast, faster and faster, soon disappearing into the distance." That was more or less the way it went. But every time he told the story, he would introduce some suspicious modifications. A-ma had preached this story as if it were the gospel truth, until one day he found out that he was not, in fact, Big Daddy Dragon's seed.

A-ma was a braggart, but everyone was fond of him. Everyone was so fascinated by his bragging that if we had a course named "The Art of Speaking", he would definitely be top of the class every year. He had a mild stutter, which in fact increased the magnetic appeal of his speech. He spoke with one hand on his hip and the other pointing proudly in the air, like a teapot. One would have mistaken him for the Great Leader in those documentary films, as if he were vowing success in the Northern Expedition in 1926, boosting morale with military mottos. Even though he was just trying to be funny, everyone admired him. When other children tried to be funny, people would think them frivolous. But when A-ma tried to be funny, everyone would call him a genius. I often thought that this must have had something to do with appearance. That look of a great leader, in such a village where people interpreted good looks as a sign of good luck, must have cultivated in him that heroic swagger.

I later realized that A-ma's heroic swagger was in fact a thorn in the flesh for my father. To understand why, you would have to know the long-standing tension between my father and Big

Daddy Dragon.

You know, in those heady days of retreat, first from the Japanese then from the Communists, my faraway motherland in Yun-nan, with all its breathtakingly beautiful and colourful scenery, used to be garrisoned with a motley assortment of competing forces, both regular troops and local militiamen, that fought a tenacious guerilla war, in that ancient motherland on the frontier of southern China. At that time, my father, who'd left college to join the army out of sheer patriotism, was left without hope of support, having to fend for himself as the leader of a militia. In the circumstances, he had no choice but to turn to the opium trade, which had once made my grandfather rich. While the different forces were fighting for territory, my father and Big Daddy Dragon, who was the son of a rural overlord, the head of the local mafia, had their first face-off. That day at dawn, my father led several local soldiers on an opium run over the Yun-fen River. One moment he heard galloping horses, the next his soldiers had been stabbed and himself captured and dragged into the woods by a group of limping, even lame petty outlaws. After he saw who he was dealing with, he glared at them out of a spirit of righteousness so vast that it filled the ancient primeval forest. "I'd say, my brothers, it is not the time for us to fight each other. We are in the same boat now. We share in our nation's glory and its shame: the blood enmity against our common enemy must always be our first priority." What happened then? According to my father, the outlaws were so moved by my father's righteousness that they not only betrayed Big Daddy Dragon but also chose to follow my father, joining his militia. My father had always believed that it was his austere righteousness that had saved him from certain death many times, offering him spiritual protection. You can still see a calligraphy scroll of lines from "The Song of the Spirit of Righteousness", by a staunch loyalist who paid for his refusal to support the Mongols after his capture by Kublai Khan with his life, hanging in our living room now. After the last retreat of all, to Taiwan, the turf war moved to the south-east corner of the island.

My dad decided to retire early when one of his militia brothers lost his mind and killed someone. He settled in this small village in a bend of the Ma-wu-k'u River. The Old Stags in the village formed a Yun-nan gang, taking the Dragon household, the Mahjong Den, as their gathering spot. My dad was too young to have a say in the group gatherings. When the bachelors picked their teeth playing Mahjong, they would ask my dad: "Where were you when I was fighting against the warlords in the Northern Expedition? Where were you when I was fighting the Japs in the Sino-Japanese War?" My dad told himself to stay calm, holding a book called *The Self-Made Man* in his hand.

The firecrackers were crackling and spluttering early in the morning of the birthday of our Great Leader. A week before, the wooden congratulations signs were already set by the sides of the only road in the village by the sea, and two weeks before other preparations for the celebration had been made. "How shall we celebrate the Great One's birthday?" someone asked in the group meeting. One replied: "How about a birthday speech?" My father nominated Big Daddy Dragon, but, having dropped out of elementary school, Big Daddy Dragon was barely literate, let alone up to writing a speech. Thus, as my highly educated and erudite father had foreseen, the honour was assigned to him. Apparently, all the Old Stags cried during the speech, and vowed to celebrate the leader's next birthday on the land that they had lost. In fact, my father's impassioned speech became a beacon for the Mahjong Den, the corruption of the Mahjong Den setting off my father's sterling character.

Father had always complained that A-chung was nothing like him, without the slightest trace of his heroic demeanour. Which had to do with why my dad didn't like Big Daddy

Dragon's son, who was born with charisma. "What use is a big head when the main thing is that it's got to look like the Great Man's?" my father said and sighed, caressing my little brother's huge bumpy head. But he was also the first to find out that A-ma was a coward, much earlier than the rest of us.

You know Mimi's and my hometown is in the south-east of this sweet potato isle? It is located on a vibrant young plate where the Central Mountain Range, the Coastal Mountain Range and the Pacific Ocean lie parallel, like a staircase. Even though there were few residents (only 2.8 per cent of the population of the island) on this narrow, backward strip of the original soil, the cultural progress, made by aboriginal myths and tales, was amazing. Driving along the road that winds down the meandering coastline, you see from time to time dense green windbreaks of whistling pine trees, each carrying itself with the unmasterable, jutting swagger of a maverick.

Mimi's and my white family compound with its spacious yard is one of these windbreaks. Ever since I can remember, I was warned: Don't ever walk inside that huge old living labyrinth of a windbreak. Of course, I have to tell you how complicated it is. Inside there are some unwelcome indigenous animals, such as snakes, which have killed sheep from A-ma's house and hens from mine. The windbreak is where we buried our wolfhound, hunting dog and spotted kitten. It is also where the Old Stags are laid to rest. And, most mysteriously, it is the final resting place of an extraordinarily beautiful, yet wretched, young woman—posthumously honoured with the name of Miss China. It is said that the whistling pine she hung herself from was soon chopped down, for fear that it had absorbed her spiritual energy and would turn into a tree demon. Miss China's ashes were buried in a water canister in the sandy bank of the creek that flows through the grove.

One day, A-ma, in high spirits, called to his followers in the village: "We've picked all the guavas in the windbreak. Let's go ask Miss China for guavas today. What do you think?" "Let's go somewhere else! It's creepy there." "What do you know? The guavas there are so big and sweet cause nobody dares to go pick them." Unable to resist temptation or the habit of deference to A-ma and obedience to his commands, they set out to visit Miss China.

It got darker and danker the deeper they walked inside. Vines wrapped around the straight trunks of the whistling pines, while bushes spread beneath. We roamed along the shallow riverbank A-ma mentioned, but didn't find a single guava tree. "It's here somewhere, the guava grove!" A-ma murmured. By that time everyone was tired of A-ma's conceit. "Yahhhhhhhhh!"

Scared out of his wits, A-ma had started yelling: "Miss China is coming! Miss China is coming!" He legged it, leading the way back to my yard. None of us, least of all A-ma, had dared to look back. "What does she look like?" someone asked, panting. A-ma, still in a panic, was pale with fear. "I saw a broken water canister. Half buried in the sand. It… it… it was Miss China!" As he spoke, my little brother A-chung was shaking his huge head. "I often go there to pick firewood. How come I've never seen Miss China before?" he asked.

It certainly was humiliating for A-ma that time. How could Miss China be a broken water canister? And this was hardly the first hit A-ma's reputation for heroism was fated to take.

4. Mimi's bewilderment

A-MA'S HEROIC MANNER WAS ALSO EXPRESSED THROUGH HIS obsession with vehicles. It started at the age of three when he got his first tricycle. Then, when he was ten, he got a bike that he exchanged for a SYM Wolf 125 cc motorcycle at sixteen. When he turned nineteen, he got his first four-wheeler. A-ma followed the same path to maturity as the history of vehicles from chariot to car, except that he traced a line of decline. Isn't materialism humanity's downfall?

This sudden revelation of A-ma's flawed character has turned into an issue for me to cogitate on in my college classes. That isn't important, as I'm now keen to rearrange some of the treacherous Mimi's secrets. Which brings me to the story of A-ma's amazing green bike.

A-ma bought this bike some time after my father purchased the very first model of the Piaggio scooter as a symbol of a self-made man. One day, on the beautiful Coastal Highway, seldom visited on foot or by car, A-ma had the idea of challenging my father and his Piaggio to a race while on his way to class. Mimi sat on the backseat of my father's scooter, but her heart had already settled on A-ma, as she kept shouting encouragements to the rhythm of his pedalling feet, which twirled faster and faster. A-ma, who looked possessed by the spirits of both dragon and horse, darted at full speed down the lonely road and snatched victory from my father, reaching the finish line a few seconds before him.

After that, Mimi started riding with A-ma. Bystanders started to spread the word of A-ma's mystical bicycle. When it reached my father, he retorted: "A-ma suddenly challenging me to a race, him riding his bike?! I know the kid likes to show off, so I kept my speed to fifty kilometres per hour, to play along. It was amusing, as if he could possibly win in a real race, ha ha."

My mother shouted "Boring" at my father, which did nothing to reduce Mimi's embarrassment at being fooled. Later, when A-ma kept on bragging about the marvels of his bike and the glory of his victory, Mimi considered time and time again telling him the truth about how a grown up fooled them.

But in those days A-ma was a bona fide, genuine hero—just take the way he protected girls. Since he was a boy, A-ma had always been a little gentleman. Before his bike turned into a joke, he looked like a rural overlord every time he rode to class.

When Mimi tapped A-ma's shoulder and said: "A-ma, my schoolbag is so heavy…" he would shoulder the whole heft of her textbooks. Once, on the train, when there was not a single seat left in the carriage, Mimi, stamping with impatience, started to complain: "A-ma, my feet hurt so bad…" A-ma immediately pointed at the little boy sitting in front of them and said: "Hey, you, stand up!" causing all the girls in the carriage to start chattering. That time, Mimi beamed with pride.

While Mimi was still wearing her hair in pigtails, Ruby, A-ma's mother, would growl at her: "Mimi! When are you going to be my daughter-in-law?" every time she went to A-ma's house by the fishpond.

Unless she was playing Mahjong, Ruby would carry out a stool and sit on the concrete in front of her house. She wore her pyjamas—a top and shorts with lace hems—out, her dishevelled hair like a bird's nest, her face fatigued; with cigarette in hand, she would sit on the bench for hours. But when she saw Mimi carrying stuff which her mum had asked her to bring over, she would leap off the bench. She could not hide her excitement as she chattered non-stop in her husky voice. "Mimi! You chubby little face, let me get a good look at you. Ah, how adorable! How I wish you would marry my son." Mimi got cuddled, patted, held, pinched—just like a puppy. But every time Mother asked: "Anyone willing to make a delivery to A-ma's house for me?" Mimi would grab the stuff and say: "I'll go!"

(Dear Mimi, I'm sorry that I can't help but reveal these secrets you have faithfully kept throughout the years. But in the course of revealing them, I realize I was piecing together the parts of you that you thought were dubious fragments. So should we continue this secret plan of ours or not?)

While most of the villagers were sceptical of Ruby, Mimi's affection for her was built upon "a common goal". Surely there were people cooking in A-ma's house—the food the Old Stags cooked was far superior to Ruby's. However, when it comes to preparing A-ma's lunchbox, it was far more important to Ruby than playing Mahjong. It was as if in these carefree days of hers, cooking for A-ma became a priority in life. Ruby would place the lunchbox into a hand-sewn bag and wait for Mimi, who in grade two still only attended afternoon classes, to come and collect it.

She also prepared two bottles of Yakult yogurt drink, one for Mimi and the other for A-ma. After some time, A-ma complained that when the Yakult reached him, the bottle cap would have a weird bulge and that the drink would be tasteless. From then on, Mimi no longer had Yakult to drink, either. From time to time, Ruby would give A-ma some pocket money, saying it was for good luck. Mimi would always rush to school before twelve when A-ma's morning classes ended. She would then tiptoe outside the window of his classroom and pass him his lunchbox, the food still warm, through the window. Since childhood, A-ma had been generous. A-ma was always there to enthuse in the windfalls and wipeouts of the Old Stags in the Mahjong Den, and the tips he got were proportionate to his enthusiasm.

With money in hand, A-ma, together with Mimi, his delivery girl, went to the grocery store to grab some instant noodles. There was a while there when my parents wondered why Mimi always looked yellowish and had no appetite. Most girls her age had started their growth spurt but Mimi never seemed to grow out of her adolescence. My parents once suspected that there were worms in Mimi's tummy, but later they found Mimi was endlessly munching on preserved food that was as yellow as her skin. My mother broke down hysterically in our courtyard. She grabbed a thin cane made of whistling pine, chased after Mimi and sent strokes down her legs. Tears and snivels covered Mimi's flushed face, and distinctive shrieks resounded through our courtyard and beyond.

"You damned child! Why don't you just get run over by a car? Look at yourself. Why don't you just die? Haven't we given you enough to eat and drink? If you like A-ma's family so much, why don't you go be their daughter?"

Apparently my mother's mean words really had their intended effect. Ruby, who was playing Mahjong across the other side of the whistling pine forest, ran over to the house as if summoned. I will have to tell you how my mother and Ruby got on one another's bad sides some other time.

But I can tell you what happened when Ruby came over that day. My mother cried and screamed herself hoarse. The woman's fatigue and febrility found temporary respite in indignant angst, under the figurative whip in my mother's bloodshot eyes. Ruby's appearance brought the tragedy to its climax. Mimi curled up on the yard of my house, which appeared to be immense at the time. Her monotonous wails were like her numb, skinny legs, which were covered in red and green welts. Mimi wanted to play dead to end the tragedy, but as soon as Ruby appeared, the dull, enervated atmosphere was revitalized. You could hear Ruby trying to calm my mother down with her coarse, indolent voice.

"She's just a kid. You can just tell her what she has done is wrong. Don't be so hard on her."

"Mrs Dragon, I don't let my kids run wild. I will regret it if I don't teach her a lesson right now. I don't want people to say that my children are spoiled."

"Okay, okay. But you only have to hit her a little bit to teach her. It won't do to hit her too much. Mimi, be a good little girl, don't cry. Go wash your face."

"What are you crying for? I'm not dead yet. Though it's not as if you'll cry when I do die. You just keep kneeling here until

I tell you. Mrs Dragon, you think I like to hit my kids? When I hit her, it is me that hurts the most. But if I don't teach them a lesson now, they'll blame you when they're older."

"All right, all right," was the only thing Ruby could say after the flood of my mother's tirade. I've wondered whether years later Ruby recalled what my mother had said about the pressure she should feel as a mother raising A-ma. "If you don't teach kids, they will hate you when they grow up." I always thought that this bit of homely wisdom, which my mother kept repeating, was her curse on A-ma and Ruby. Along with a story she was always telling. The story was about a man who hated his mother for not teaching him a lesson when he was young, causing him to make one mistake after another. When he was about to be executed, he begged to suck his mother's milk for one last time but bit his mother's nipple off instead.

(Mimi, do you also suspect this story was just made up to give my mother an excuse for her excess when she savages us with her whistling pinewood cane? Or might she really have a superpower allowing her to predict the future, by virtue of which she was making a prophecy? If so, do you think her prophecy will come true, and A-ma is going to end up tearing off Ruby's dry dugs, gore at the corners of his mouth?)

It took A-ma a long time to get up the courage to step into my house again. Every time he saw my mum he greeted her and bowed respectfully and attentively. You know, my mum had this strange ability to order the cabbage heads in the village to help clean up our house. But A-ma, without having to be asked, would take the broom and start sweeping our yard. To get on my mum's good side, he even started to eat pork at the table, shamelessly! A-ma's family, in the days they lived on the south-western frontier of China, had been recorded as non-Han in the last census before 1949. Big Daddy Dragon, who was hui and therefore a Muslim, strictly followed the religious prohibition against eating pork. In order to show their respect for Big Daddy Dragon, the stags, the veteran bachelors in the Mahjong Den, never put pork on the table. Now you saw A-ma tasting all the pork dishes on ours: pig ear, pig knuckle, pig rib, pig heart, pig liver, pig kidney, pig tripe—A-ma enjoyed all parts of a pig, as if he was feasting upon some kind of ambrosia. Satisfied, my mother asked: "Tasty?"

"Delicious!"

"Aren't you scared that your dad will get mad?"

"No!" A-ma said, licking his oily lips and patting his huge belly.

All the Old Stags said that A-ma wasn't afraid of anything, except my mum. When she heard, my mum couldn't be happier. "Oh, really?" she said, full of herself.

After that, Mimi didn't have any Yakult to drink or snack noodles to eat. Ruby used the bottles of Yakult as the body and some knitting wool as the outfit to make baby dolls, which she put into Mimi's school bag. Squeezing Mimi's cheek, she said: "You can't change your mind since you accepted my gift. You have to marry my son when you grow up."

Mimi, you thought to yourself at that moment: "If only the two mums could change places!" How ungrateful you were!

5. Engagement at sweet sixteen

MIMI LEFT THE TWO DOLLS MADE WITH YAKULT BOTTLES on the cabinet until she burnt them on the sand in the windbreak at the age of fourteen. Tongues of flame spread by the wind raked left and right beside her feet before morphing into amoebae breeding and dying in the crackling fire. The melted bottles had a peculiarly pungent smell, which made the whistling pines dizzy as well.

That year, Mimi grew into a bitter young woman. She sat on the swing my father built and listened to the wind flirt with the trees. The weight of secrets suddenly a load on her mind, she poured them out to the whistling pines as she swung. My pet, Hero the wolfhound, padded close and licked her pale, dangling legs with his black spotted tongue when she stopped moving. She leaned down and embraced the sympathetic creature, leaving him covered in tears and snivel. That year, Hero washed himself much more often than usual, like he'd known all along.

Mimi grew into a melancholy young woman. When you saw her walking in our yard, it was hard to connect this little woman with the image of a flat-chested, straight-hipped, monkey-like girl of half a year before. But she didn't welcome her development. It was too late, she muttered under her breath, a lyric of sorrow heard only by Hero's sharp brown ears.

Since the news of A-ma's engagement spread, Mimi had seemed ill as she wrestled with her inner demons, afflicted by remorse. It all started when A-ma fled the monkey-like Mimi's childish circle. A-ma shot up incredibly like Popeye on spinach, and received tons of compliments from the Old Stags. White T-shirt and blue shorts were so tight on his muscular body that his robust legs seemed ready to burst the seams at any time. Mimi, who had cut her plaits, still went to school on the first bus with A-ma every morning. Squeezed in the bus on the bumpy road, Mimi, who didn't even reach the height of A-ma's shoulders, stood beside him as if beside a wall. She held his arm as she was unable to reach the handles, and her head rocked when the bus lurched, bumping against A-ma's smelly and sweaty chest. The strong odour made her giddy and drowsy. She looked up at his sprouting moustache and small red pimples, seeing the muddled physical maturity with affection and revulsion.

When Mimi was still wearing her hair in plaits she would deliver food to A-ma, and after she cut her hair short she delivered mail. The first time Mimi delivered mail for A-ma during lunch break, he took the opportunity to climb over the school wall with Mimi and have a bowl of stinky tofu at the street vendor's. A-ma told Mimi again and again to be especially careful when she sent his letters, so as not to let her form teacher Ms Hsu find out. He also told Mimi in a threatening tone that if she got caught, they would all have to stand on the platform in front of the field or hold a stool above their heads in class or get a major demerit on their report cards.

The letters Mimi surreptitiously delivered were love letters, to a girl named Mei-chih. Years later, Mimi could no longer remember the pretty girl's face but couldn't forget that instant humiliation. I was like a child on a jaunt out of my childish world, gawking around, captivated by adult sex appeal. It was like a powerful beam of light that illuminated my jealousy, leaving me no place to hide. After all I could not enter that world to which A-ma now belonged. Mei-chih's ample bosom, exquisite waist and round bottom, along with A-ma's sour odour and rough voice, set off the tardiness of my own maturation and the fact that I had been forgotten. I was fated to be the one who chose to leave, most unwillingly.

Mei-chih's friendliness was taken as the oblivious patronizing disrespect of the adult world towards children. Especially when Mei-chih stroked Mimi with a beautiful smile saying: "You're A-ma's little sister Mimi? So cute!" Mimi immediately, and without a second thought, mimicked the Old Stags and under her breath told Mei-chih, who thought she had the advantage with her soft white hands: "Fuck yer mother's cunt."

At first, Mimi was just a message girl. When A-ma and Mei-chih started dating, Mimi became a tagalong. Every day after school, she would follow them everywhere, dwarfed by her big backpack. She would miss the first school bus she had to catch to make the first class and the last bus after guidance class in the afternoon, thereby missing dinner. Neither of them paid her any attention, just sweet-talked each other in the most revoltingly soppy way imaginable in front of Mimi, as if she didn't know any better. Disgusted, Mimi said: "A-ma, let's go home. We're about to miss the bus."

A-ma replied pleasantly: "Just a minute." But the more dates he went on the more he tended to lose his temper. "Mimi, can't you just go home yourself? Why do you have to wait for me?" "I always come to school and get out of school with you. If I go home alone, what would your mother think?" When you saw A-ma holding Mei-chih's hand walking along the east coast with the sun sinking into the mountains, or playing around in the town called Newport, also known as Success, their shadows stretched long, and the adult figures belonged to A-ma and Mei-chih, the little one to Mimi. Mimi was clearly aware of how awkward it was, a scene of two adults with a child tagging along, well before she heard A-ma's exasperated exclamation: "Mimi, can you not be such a pest? I can't do anything with you around."

If you were there you would have seen Mimi, like a little ant, her way forward blocked as if by a mean child, actually turn around without saying a word. She chose to leave.

A-ma's engagement at sixteen years old was exhilarating, as much fun as playing house. One day, A-ma came up with the idea and grabbed his mother Ruby by her plump waist. "Ma, I want to get married." "Married?" Marriage: a word that reminded Ruby of her long forgotten teenage dreams. In Ruby's uneducated lexicon, marriage meant the reproduction of race and life and the meaning of an alliance with a lover. A dream that never came true for her had very considerately but unintentionally been fulfilled by A-ma. She stroked A-ma affectionately on his Great Man's head.

"Marriage? Yup, getting married is good. My A-ma is in love! But why not bring her home and let me meet her first?"

So A-ma brought Mei-chih home to meet the family. And the Old Stags, who came out of the Mahjong Den to see what was happening in the irresistible real-life game of house. Marathon, who was good at making pea powder and had been living in A-ma's house for a long time, said: "My father took me wife-seeking on a donkey when I was only twelve years old."

Grandpa Shou with his big flappy ears also took the chance to retell his amorous tales, which everyone had heard a million times already. "Those Dai aboriginal maidens don't wear knickers. Every time I walked by the river they'd lift up their skirts filled with mussels. Oolala, I got so shy!"

Of course, you could hear some criticism as well. Weirdo Yang, famous for his eccentricity, who was also from an ethnic minority and lived next door to A-ma, sat on a big rattan chair under an old tree and watched coldly while tapping his bamboo cane. "What's that bitch Ruby up to now? The Dragons will fail in her hands sooner or later." And Busybody Chang, who never missed a chance to be snarky, said: "Falling in love when they should be studying, what a couple of useless teenagers."

Big Daddy Dragon said nothing at first. He sat in the Mahjong Den and rubbed the tiles. He remained silent even when Mei-chih came to the house. The first time Ruby met Mei-chih, she gave her a gold ring and praised her, that with her full figure and guileless smile she looked lucky. Even though his father had high hopes for A-ma, who was only in grade nine, Ruby didn't see it that way. Without any urgency, she coaxed Big Daddy Dragon: "Old man Dragon, how many years do you have to be picky about your future daughter-in-law? You can only hold your grandchild in your arms if you're alive, am I right? After A-ma gets engaged, he'll settle down and study hard! Don't you think?"

So how happily ever after did it turn out? Not happily at all, or ever after. It ended with Big Daddy Dragon's angry monster's roar, "RI-DI-CU-LOUS!" It was so loud that you can still hear it now above the whistling pines during a thunderstorm.

Nope, A-ma didn't end up getting married. He even failed to gain admission to any college in the nation, not even the worst. He enlisted in the army, got his head shaved. Mei-chih, after the engagement was broken off, went to the west and worked her way through a co-op programme, finally becoming a bride and having several kids. A-ma never saw her again.

Mimi, if I told you you were the winner in this heartbreaking love triangle, would you believe me? When I recollected our conversations, when I was desperate to read your shadowy history to piece together your fragmentary memories, to rearrange your multifarious potential, I felt the tiniest bit ashamed of my reprehensible urge to probe someone else's wounds, expose their scars, appropriating everything for my art. That's why I should come clean to you by writing my confessions. It was all done out of childish pique. Mimi, please remember these words. It had something to do with my friend Uncle Dumdum, the little thief who reeked with the decrepit sour sweat of an old crook, reminding me of the dinosaurs, the permanently elected members, in the national assembly that we, the wild lilies, demonstrated against just a few years ago. Always pestering me to enter into a blood pact with him, he ended up selling me out. Mimi, you know what? I was so lost and confused that I fell to the nadir of my life. Only one short story in the past year. Dumped by two boyfriends in six months. Friends close to me all blamed me in the guise of concern. I apologized to everyone who appeared in my nightmares.

I began to fool around with a pack of fair-weather friends in the Celestial Retreat, where we all sat around talking about rarefied subjects like literature. (It was interesting that everyone there had just lost in love.) My buddy Uncle Dumdum, with his bodhisattva's heart of pure gold, was so nice that he wasted his time conciliatorily drinking with me and listening with abnormal patience to me as I shed drunken tears and snivel and whinged about my depression and my sorrow (which, surprisingly, my Celestial buddies had long heard too many times to care about any more). So, I invited him on a trip to the east coast to show my appreciation. Moved by the mystic beauty of my hometown, he wrote a masterpiece into which he poured his soul and told me: "You're Mimi." How could Mimi be me? Sullied by an old veteran, she had eight boyfriends, collecting men like guns. Men such as an overseas student who fought a guerrilla war with the Communists, an Irish Republican soldier who smoked weed, and a playboy who liked to hold the flag high in protest marches but was actually a coward. She even had a sketchy relationship with the author.

"This isn't me."

"Yes, it is. Mimi's spirit is yours."

"What do you know?"

"Right, that's what I mean. That's Mimi's attitude."

And you heard our teacher, who wanted us to turn in our assignments and couldn't stand our arguments, say: "Why don't you two just get married?" Say whuh? Huh?!

Mimi, did you lay down your weapons upon understanding my predicament? Did you show me the slightest sympathy, I, a pathetic artist sunk so deep in the mire of writer's block I had no choice but to expose your private affairs? Just like the sympathy I felt for you after licking your wounds in the course of exposing you?

6. The mystery of mortality

LAST AUTUMN, I STARTED WALKING STEP BY STEP INTO THE trap Mimi had laid for me. This spring, when my teacher was resorting to all means possible for me to hand in my draft, Mimi told me: "You are me." And I forced myself to actually believe I was really Mimi. But how did I manage to make Mimi think that I was the incarnation of her existence in this world? I've started suspecting that I am just a mere chess piece placed by Mimi in the human realm.

If I were a mere pawn, maybe when I record a drama that had been played out, when I confront issues like mortality, it would all be easier to bear.

In our hometown, the word "death" was far from unfamiliar to Mimi and me. From the moment fear awakened for the very first time onwards, following a seasonal cycle like migratory birds, the deaths of the aged veterans were like the falling of the needles of the whistling pines. But considering that the fall and rebirth of the whistling pines is the perpetuation of a natural self-sufficient equilibrium, what kind of rebirth, then, would spawn from the demise of the veterans?

Like many other veterans, my father settled down in a small village near the Ma-wu-k'u after his retirement from the military, which was a result of the law of collective punishment and disappointment with his career prospects. He packed himself and his dependent on the special little diesel train from the hot and noisy city in the north to the wild territory "behind the mountains" on the east coast. Thereupon I started pondering the millennial history of my family and discovered that "exodus" had flowed in the blood in my ancestors' veins for aeons. Since the dawn of our lineage in the Loess Plateau of Northern China, through the fecund and populous basin of the Yangtze River, to the ancient malaria-infested kingdom of Dali, my forebears accomplished peregrinations, passing a peripatetic heritage on to my father. However, my father has outdone even his own father in the past few dozen years, not only completing his own emigration but also, in the prime of his youth, claiming his own turf as an enclave in a sovereign nation and fighting several beautiful guerrilla battles. While comparing my family's development with A-ma's own glorious family history, I quickly realized my blood's superior vigour. With every relocation, our family enjoyed several generations of prosperity. However, in the area ruled by A-ma's family, great prosperity gradually turned into misery. A-ma's forefathers were local thugs who lorded it over a small patch of Yunnan until his grandfather agreed to sell his ancestors' land in exchange for an official post: he became an illiterate county governor, but didn't keep the county for his son. Big Daddy Dragon fought a turf war on the frontier of China and Burma, an alien realm to most Chinese, while A-ma's last stronghold turned out to be the Mahjong Den, which is where I left him. I have come to believe that my decision to leave my hometown and eventually my island home for further education was merely an ancestral summons flowing in my blood to carry on our glorious family tradition.

At first my father lived in the village, taking over Papa Wang's grocery store on the public road, which is where I formed my initial impression of death. I hid inside the store beneath the window and peeped at a funeral procession down the gravel road, until my mother found us kids and locked us up in the darkness of the kitchen, her two hands pressing roughly down on our heads as she yelled: "You're not allowed to watch." But I did, I saw it approach. I could almost smell a rotten odour and the dust kicked up by the procession floating in the air. Intrigued by the deafening clatter, I stood on my tiptoes and squeezed a glimpse. I saw in the procession of male pall bearers, their white headscarves soaked with sweat, my father and three uncles struggling under the huge brown coffin, making slow progress. My mother said that the dead man lying inside was Chao Junior, who had left over a hundred thousand dollars to the children of veterans of the resistance against Japan and the Chinese Civil War. I myself got a couple of thousand dollars from him in scholarship money every year when I was in college.

That evening, my father came home grim-faced. He said nothing at the dinner table. We ragamuffins wanted him to satisfy our curiosity about what we had seen that day, but he just sat there expressionlessly.

"Eat your dinner" was all that he said.

My mother was still angry at us for our recalcitrant peeping.

"Still up to no good? Haven't I punished you enough for one day? If you don't want to eat, go and stand by the wall."

When we went to bed, I heard my father and mother talking in a whisper:

"Tomorrow morning we're going to the grave to lay the concrete. We cut down another few whistling pines. It won't do to keep encroaching on a public windbreak."

"I think if they don't formally approve the public cemetery, that's what the windbreak's going to become."

Then I heard my father ask for a back massage.

"Big Daddy Dragon sure knows how to order people around, like he thinks he's still a petty warlord in Yun-nan. He doesn't do anything himself, just tells people to do things. I didn't get any rest all day. Ow ow ow! It hurts here and here and here. When he dies see who wants to carry his coffin."

The deaths of the bachelor veterans spread like the plague many years after my family moved into the windbreak and took on a custodial role—the role of forester. Their deaths one after another were like the falling of the needles of the whistling pines, but in the moment the needles hit the ground, you could hear the sandy ground issue a quiet sigh. Big Daddy Dragon's demise was the climax of the music of mortality, which began with a weird metallic impact and ended with a great rending. Then there was nothing, not the slightest muffled lament to break the silence. The line of life and death was redrawn by these sudden fallings to earth. At the time the elders were paying constant attention to each other's appearances. "Watch out, your face's all red," they would say.

There were far fewer empty bottles of rice wine of a day, and Ruby the hostess bought a blood pressure reader. When they were at loose ends the ageing bachelors would take the stool in front of her to check their systolic and diastolic. Ruby just never expected she'd lose that husband of hers. His face wasn't red, he didn't drink much, but he ended up leaving this world in exactly the same way as Chao Junior. When his head hit the concrete, life left him, just like that.

Death in the Mahjong Den began with the cook Marathon. Had he not behaved so idiotically all the time, he might have been saved from a spiritual trip to the Western Heavens the second time he fell into A-ma's fishpond. That night, in their dreams, old Pappy Shou and Busybody Chang both heard Marathon's gratingly hoarse drunkard's voice. For a while he clucked like a cock. For a while he barked like a dog. His ever-shoeless feet, which had two-centimetre-thick calluses, flip-flopped on the cement pavement around the fishpond. Pappy Shou could tell Marathon was running around the pond with a bottle of rice wine in his hand.

"Hey! You really think it's a marathon, don't you? Don't expect me to fish you out if you fall into the pond again."

Busybody Chang wasn't so kind. His nose poking at the screen over the window at the bed, he scolded him, spittle flying.

"Fuck you! Son of a bitch! We still need to sleep even if you don't!"

First there was the crashing sound of the bottle. Then, a splash. Pappy Shou and Busybody Chang giggled when they heard it. "Son of a bitch!" they said, at the same time, then both went back to bed and fell asleep again.

In the morning, a fierce screaming woke the old bachelors who lived around the Mahjong Den. Running out in their loose boxers, these bachelors, still sleepy, thought the horn had sounded for them to retake the mainland from the

Communists. As soon as they saw Marathon's body, strong as an ox when it was alive, floating dead in the fishpond, its skin having turned from swarthy to purplish-grey, their excited faces contorted all of a sudden. Among them, you saw Pappy Shou and Busybody Chang blubbering, slapping themselves and stamping their feet.

"Wake up, Marathon! It's not funny anymore! You son of a bitch! Wake up!"

The bachelors divided up the tasks, preparing for the wake. They fished out the body, bought ice blocks, prepared the corpse for the coffin and cleaned up. A crowd of fat carps also died in Marathon's memory when the water was drained. Pappy Shou and Busybody Chang did nothing but shake Marathon desperately, until black blood flowed from his eyes.

Big Daddy Dragon bawled: "Stop crying! Get to work!"

This time Busybody Chang was emboldened, like he'd eaten bear heart and leopard liver. He bawled back: "It's all you! You dug the fucking pond for your son, at the cost of my brother's life. A curse on your family! May none of them die a good death. Let the son ruin you, the wife screw around on you!"

The day Marathon died, two old men started brawling, Busybody Chang and Big Daddy Dragon.

The second death in the Mahjong Den was far more peaceful. Weirdo Yang, who lived in the eastern room of A-ma's house, fell to the ground while he was watering plants in the garden. He never had much to do with anyone. Had it not been for A-ma, it might have taken days for someone to notice. A-ma had slipped out of the military academy that day and tiptoed into Yang's garden thinking nobody was there. He wanted to steal some of Yang's big mangos.

Weirdo Yang passed away peacefully, but the eastern room he left provoked a crisis in the Mahjong Den. Who's gonna move into this room? Big Daddy Dragon found it hard to make a fair judgement. At last, on Ruby's suggestion, he kept it for Chou Shih-yung, who had been away from the Mahjong Den for ten years and was coming back.

"He has followed you through thick and thin since he was ten or so. When you got to Taiwan, you didn't help him get settled like an elder brother should. Don't turn your back on honour now that you're old. I bumped into him on the street the last time I went to see your son. He's been travelling around, saving some money. He said he'd better come back now that he's got old. Brothers should keep each other company and take care of each other."

This sent Big Daddy Dragon over the edge. Dragon slapped himself on the chest and blustered: "I, Flying-Cloud of the Dragon Clan, have nothing in my breast but a spirit of brotherhood. If this lad Chou Shih-yung hadn't carried me on his back for a whole three days in the woods when we were running for our lives, I might have been a goner. Next time you visit A-ma, ask Chou to come back. I will keep the room for him."

Every member of the Mahjong Den was indignant. Old age must have befuddled the old dragon's brain. Everyone knew why Ruby went west so often. Those excuses—visiting A-ma, taking care of her old mother—only idiots would believe her. How did Big Daddy Dragon become such an old fool? Was he a man or a mouse?

On the day Big Daddy Dragon passed away, his speech was so exceptionally clear that Mimi claimed to overhear everything. With his hands behind his back, Big Daddy Dragon was pacing in the courtyard on the concrete ground. He looked like his father the illiterate magistrate handling county business, none too bright yet impressive. His monologue was lengthy, but even-tempered, a vast contrast to the heated conflict with his son and wife the night before. Mimi said Big Daddy Dragon's attitude towards his son's occupation appeared to have softened. He probably regretted kicking A-ma out and forcing him to go back to what A-ma described as a "big prison".

"Look at me, see what I have gone through!" It was the second time that A-ma had slipped away from the military academy. Unlike the first time, Big Daddy Dragon was no longer inclined to try to reason with him. He rolled up a trouser leg, grabbed A-ma's Great Man's bald head, which was some twenty centimetres higher than his, and said: "Look at my leg, a bullet pierced it!" He was pointing at the scar that looked like a withered flower on his leg. Then, he pulled up his shirt and stuck out his belly. "See? Shot by a bullet, bang!" He gave A-ma's bare head a slap. "You can't even take a bit of training. Where are your guts?" He stretched out his hand to give A-ma another slap on the face. A-ma nimbly avoided it.

"Dad, you don't understand at all. I don't like military academy life. It doesn't suit me, neither. Why force me?"

"Bah! What do you know? If I had gone to military academy, I would have done much better in Taiwan. After all, I was a general of the guerillas! They dismissed all my military achievements when I got here, just because I never went to school. In the end they thought they could shut me up with a measly sergeant major assignment. I want you to go to military academy and become an officer. It's all for the sake of your future."

"If you really were thinking on my behalf, you wouldn't force me."

"Nonsense! Studying in military academy will give you a bright future. When we retake the mainland, A-ma, you'll have your chances. Wartime's the best time to rise through the ranks!" Big Daddy Dragon's furious and contorted face turned sweet when he fell into his favourite daydream.

"We'll never retake the mainland. Old Chiang is dead. Everyone now says 'Let the Three Principles of the People Reunify China'."

"Aiya! Outrageous! You traitor to family and country!

He's Old Chiang now, is he?" Big Daddy Dragon roared as he chased Ma around the yard, kicking and punching him.

At that moment, as usual, Ruby came out and separated the glaring roosters young and old. She stood in front of A-ma to protect him.

"Hey, young people have their own ways of thinking. Why does he have to think as you do? There's no point forcing him to do what he doesn't want to. I told you before: A-ma is doing well—too well to go to a military academy. He's not—"

Before she finished, Big Daddy Dragon shouted again: "Damn, bitch! You don't know shit!"

Busybody Chang, who was drawing water from the well, stood there for quite a while before he put down his carrying pole, came over and said: "Ruby, you don't understand. A-ma, listen to me: when I was captured and drafted at fifteen or sixteen, I resented it for a while and was definitely not used to life in the barracks. I cried every night, just like you, and I even ran away. But soon I went back and got used to it. Just hurry up and get used to it."

"You only went back because you couldn't find anything to eat," A-ma said.

"You smart-aleck! You're going back tonight. Right after dinner. If you stay here a minute longer, I'll punch you till you piss yourself. Pussy! I won't stand for a useless son," Big Daddy Dragon shouted.

That night while A-ma rushed back to the academy, Big Daddy Dragon stayed up pacing in the yard. The next morning he was still pacing back and forth, and no one knew what he was thinking. Only Mimi noticed how red his face was, how shiny with sweat his forehead. Sunshine fell gently on him, bringing warmth, and even Mimi, who stood over ten metres away, could feel the heat steaming off his body. A short while later he fell down hard on the concrete like a gunshot, and he didn't move again.

It was the dishevelled Chou Shih-yung who first rushed out of the house.

Eventually, my father shouldered the main work of Big Daddy Dragon's burial. This was the last time for the old bachelors to carry a coffin and to dig a grave. After that, death spread like a plague in the village. As more and more old men died, there were fewer and fewer to carry coffins, so the labour of burial fell to the undertaker. The old bachelors would say over and over, I'm old, can't lift it no more. Their words gradually became slurred, as if their memories had returned to dreams, like Mimi came walking in and out of my dreams.

7. Your unquiet blood flows in my veins

A COUPLE OF WRAITHS WERE GOING AT IT, PERFORMING that old fighting demons skit, in the windbreak.

A man and a woman, both naked. Their loose skin and coarse wrinkles betrayed their advanced age.

They had found a safe and comfortable place sheltered by the whistling pines. There, the pine needles had covered the sandy ground, forming a bed, while the undergrowth and grass worked as curtains. Sweating, man and woman were lying on the twigs and needles, which emitted the uniquely cool and dry scent of pine. A gust of cool wind blew through the woods, rustling the needles. Aside from the rustling sound, moans and groans and exclamations like "Oh Bro" and "Dear Sis!" were heard. Upon hearing these sounds, the sheep that were grazing at the outer ring of the windbreak started bleating in time with the yelps.

That day, my father, the forester of the whistling pine grove, did his routine patrol. As he inspected whether the newly grown royal palm trees had been trampled down by the sheep grazing nearby, he heard their raving voices. He crept towards the sound on his belly, the same way he crept through primeval forests as a guerilla fighter in the old days of his youth. He approached cautiously, for fear of alerting the people there and, in turn, losing his life. "Gosh!" he almost yelled out when he saw the scene—a man and a woman were tangled together, both of them in the buff! Because of the perspiration, the needles, long and thin, were stuck to their exposed skin, and tendrils of their stringy, messed-up hair dangled in front of their faces, which expressed a mixture of the ecstasy of death and the pain of rebirth. Their movements stunned Father even more. The woman climbed onto the man and started quivering as if she were struck by lightning. Later she lay under the man, and took the man's dick into her wide mouth as if she hadn't had any in years. Father couldn't move, nor could he speak. He was completely dumbfounded. The sheep grazing nearby took no notice, treading on Father as if he were a log on the ground. In great pain, Father fought back the urge to scream.

"Better let sleeping dogs lie." Back home, he told my mum all he saw in the woods, sparing no detail, but also that he'd decided not to spread the news, for fear of stirring up trouble. "It's their own business," he said.

My mum seemed like she had finally got the goods on Ruby. She raised her voice and said: "See! I knew she was dirty. Just look at where she came from! It just goes to show that a dog can't help eating shit. Your compatriots over there in the Mahjong Den are so easy to fool! All she needs to do is join in the game, have some drinks with them, cook some dishes, and take their blood pressure, and they talk to her so sweet, like she's the sinner that became a saint. But if I were dirty like she is, I'd be wary if I heard people praise me like that." So far my mother's stress was on moral hygiene, but her speech soon turned into self-pity.

"I guard the woods, do the housework, and teach the kids the difference between right and wrong, and who notices me or thinks to praise me? Why am I working so hard? What do I get from these deeds? I play the bad cop when she enjoys herself. She eats, drinks, does what she wants, and sleeps around, yet people still think she's the best. What do I get from working so hard?"

Weirdly enough, though the whole incident had nothing to do with Mother, she ended up weeping.

"Not again." Mimi raised her eyebrows, shrugged her shoulders, went to her room and slammed the door. Bam!

"Aiya… Look at your daughter. What's with her attitude? She thinks highly of Ruby and would rather be her child. What's wrong with me? I don't gamble or steal. And does she appreciate me? Does she know she should feel proud of having me as her mum?" she said, starting to sob again.

Chou Shih-yung returned to the Mahjong Den, like a vigorous city lad. Whenever he played Mahjong, it was go big or go home. The cigarettes he smoked had to be President brand. Unlike the Old Stags, who wore sweatshirts with dark grey trousers, he was fastidious about his attire. He also made sure his hair was well groomed—sleek and glossy. Nonetheless, he was serious about his work. After Marathon's death, Chou Shih-yung took on some of the chores. Every day he would graze the three dozen-odd sheep that A-ma's family kept in the windbreak.

When he was done with his chores, he would make his hometown's famous dish. However, his peameal cakes were neither as fragrant nor as tender as Marathon's. He was also not as hard-working as Marathon, who would wake up as early as three to grind the peas. Marathon, with an awful husky voice, would sing weird songs that woke people from sleep. For her part, Ruby started to do some of the cooking. Every day, she would go to the windbreak to deliver a lunchbox to Chou Shih-yung.

On the day Big Daddy Dragon hit his head and died, Chou

Shih-yung scurried out from the room that was decorated with beaded curtains and whence the scent of Famous Star-brand floral water would occasionally emanate. He was pulling up his underwear—white underwear patterned with blue stars. It was different from the stretched and faded army underwear the other Old Stags wore. With his underwear hiked up his thighs, he ran towards Big Daddy Dragon shouting: "Brother Lung! Brother Dragon! Are you okay?!"

No, the room Chou Shih-yung scurried out from was not the dank one Weirdo Yang had left behind. You've probably figured out by now who acted out the demon fight, who starred in the hot, steamy, racy scene my father had witnessed in the windbreak.

Not long after Big Daddy Dragon's death, Chou Shih-yung officially moved into A-ma's house. Strange that no one stood up for Big Daddy Dragon, with the exception of my father, who suggested in a meeting that the substantial inheritance in Ruby's hands and the plot of land which everyone had chipped in to buy be left for A-ma's education. Other than that, Ruby had the right to decide how the remaining money would be spent. However, everyone would be able to monitor her spending, a right Ruby would be unable to gainsay. There was a tacit consensus that A-ma should be left with some means of subsistence. Ruby had long lost the trust of the others, and other than Big Daddy Dragon, nobody treated Chou Shih-yung like a brother. Although no one spoke up, they all felt a certain uneasiness.

Everyone knows that bitch and that scrounger were the death of Big Daddy, who swallowed his pride out of fraternal loyalty. And see how that bastard Chou Shih-yung rewards his brother's loyalty! He has the gall to sow his wild oats in his brother's field! And that's what did it. Big Daddy could be angry with A-ma all day long without his blood pressure crossing the red line, but who could he turn to to vent about this? Yes, Big Daddy is dead because he kept his feelings bottled up inside. Right.

You saw Old Stags sitting on deck chairs under the trees, resting and cooling themselves with paper fans. They had been discussing it for quite a while, but none of them could explain the root cause of Big Daddy's sudden death. All they knew was the cause of death was a brain aneurysm, which struck like a contagious disease. He died just like Marathon and Weirdo Yang.

Ruby repaid the military academy for A-ma's keep with a hundred and thirty thousand dollars, all the money that Big Daddy Dragon had left behind. The same way Big Daddy Dragon had redeemed her from the stews. Even though she could say that she had turned over a new leaf, the stain was there forever. A-ma dropped out of the academy and soon got labelled a Grade A rogue. My father bailed him out of jail several times, which took twice the effort as bailing a normal person out, all because of that conspicuous red stamp on his record. "Save some effort and send him to the juvenile reformatory!" Instead of being persuaded, the police officers usually tried to talk my father out of it.

Ruby had left the brothel at least a decade before, but had never won acceptance with the folks from my closed, conservative hometown. It went against the ideology with which they had been inculcated and their whole philosophy of life. As my mother had said: "A dog can't help eating its own shit." Let's assume Ruby and Chou Shih-Yung forged a transcendent bond, but who would believe that a whore could feel true love? My mother had insulted her on purpose, merely because of the jealous nature of a woman. Like all traditional women, my mother sought perfection, working her fingers to the bone to manage our household and raise us right. No wonder she would feel upset when a woman who in her eyes was anything but perfect (even a shameless hussy) criticized her for being too strict with her children. (In Ruby's words, "Like how she treats her enemies.") "What right does she have?" my mother repeatedly reminded us of the condemned man who bit off his mother's nipple as if she were a fortune teller rubbing an amethyst. "To see where a child came from just look at his mother, he he he," she snickered.

Mimi, you would surely feel disturbed by her prophecy. You were still so young and in your mind Ruby was the model of a loving mother. She used to press her warm and soft breast against you and rock little you in her lap. She would pinch your cheek and waist and ask: "Ah hah! When are you going to be my daughter-in-law?" You recall that every time you crossed the street with Mother, she would reach out a finger for your little palm to grasp, but you would always lose your grip because it was clammy, which would get you an abrupt painful pinch.

You envied A-ma when you saw Ruby giving him a bath, teasing him for running around covered in nothing but soap. "How shameless, asking your mother to bathe you at the age of twelve." Crouching beside the well, you watched and giggled. How happy they were, mother and son. Our mother almost never looked happy in front of us.

To this day you're still confused as to why you often wet the bed as a girl or why you'd get a beating from Mother when you woke up shivering in the damp. So you silently resisted Mother's prophecy about A-ma and came over to visit me, pretending to be tough and telling me: no matter what the truth turns out to be, and what turns out to be fantasy, you can't just listen to people sigh out loud, you also have to have a certain degree of sympathy.

After Big Daddy Dragon's death, we didn't see as much grief in A-ma as we'd expected, or any sense of purpose. Instead of mourning, he bought a huge motorcycle with the remainder of the fortune Big Daddy Dragon had left, the last of his inheritance, and roared down the Coastal Highway all day long. Now he would disdain the notion of a race with my father's antique Piaggio scooter. Chasing the wind, pursuing the sun, was A-ma's newest dream, and was all he wanted to do. He wore his hair long, covering his stunning Great Man's head. He removed the muffler on his huge Wolf.

If you walk along the beautiful Coastal Highway and sense the thundering of an engine and the swift wind passing by with a loud roar, and haven't figured out what's going on, remember not to get angry and curse "Shit", "Fuck yer mama" or "Boring!" or the like when you see a column of blue fumes and long hair fluttering in the wind. If you do, you'll see A-ma pull a U-turn and charge with eyes as wild as a wolf's, one leg pawing the ground to up his acceleration. And just when you think you're a goner, A-ma'll slam on the brakes, stop right in front of you, and spit at you, his face twisted with anger. He'll stutter the way he always does when he talks to strangers. "G, g, got a problem?" "Fu, fu, fuck yer mama's cunt!"

Apparently, wolves are nocturnal animals. A-ma was born under the sign of the dragon (his family name) and horse (the sign he got from birth, in addition to being the second of the characters in his given name). Now he regarded himself as a wolf. But what's with all these animals among his associates? No wonder Big Daddy Dragon was always rebuking him while he was still alive—worse than a beast! A-ma started living a nocturnal life, not waking up till noon. At night, he and his friends from the neighbouring villages gathered on the Coastal Highway near the Mahjong Den. Sounds of wine bottles clinking could be heard now and then along with howling and laughter, destroying the tranquillity of the village night. Busybody Chang, who lived closest to the Coastal Highway, suffered countless sleepless nights because of the terrible noise.

"Oh Lordy, he's totally lawless, out of control. The whole family has been running wild since Big Daddy's death. And if the rafters aren't even, the beams must be crooked: A-ma is the same as Ruby." It was just like what my mother said. "Well, no wonder. The same blood flows in their veins," I said to Mimi.

8. A-ma, don't cry

MIMI, DO YOU STILL REMEMBER THAT EARLY SUMMER NIGHT, when the rich fragrance of seven-mile spice wafted through the air and squirrels danced among the branches of the whistling pines? You were drowsy, befuddled, but your formidable will urged you to hold on, for you had to meet everyone's expectations for you to get good grades in the coming high school entrance exams. Your textbooks were densely packed with red and blue letters bouncing and blurring in your tired eyes, bullying them and giving you premature dark circles, so you fought back the only way you could, by drooling rudely over them. Suddenly, you seemed to hear the melancholy melody of a bamboo flute coming from the forest. You recalled Weirdo Yang, who they said was an enthusiastic maker, performer and bestower of bamboo flutes, who only showed kindness to the children of your family, and who had once given you a freshly carved bamboo flute, years ago. You remembered that you held your breath in your cheeks until it ached, and blew so hard that you even spat a little in the bamboo tube, its wood still fresh and wet, but the only thing you blew was a loud fart. But since Weirdo Yang had died a year ago, whence this beautiful melancholy melody? The Old Stags said that Weirdo Yang was back. Though they didn't like the old fool, they could never stop weeping upon hearing his nocturne. "He's back!" they told each other.

That night, at the same time as the veterans were listening to the strains of a distant flute, Mimi heard the giggles and howls of A-ma's "friends" coming from the Coastal Highway.

"No, he's not worth it anymore, that lazy bones A-ma. He will never be my prince charming…" she grumbled in the stupor of her drowsiness. However, just a couple of years ago, A-ma always came to my place to cram whenever there was a test around the corner. "What a nice arrangement, Mimi can motivate him to study harder," said Big Daddy Dragon. But that lazy pig A-ma would never make it through half of the English words before falling asleep on our bed, snoring like a bear, and always waking up my father, who would get up for a pee. "That A-ma! Shame on him," my father often said, sighing and shaking his head.

"A-ma! Get up!" Mimi shook A-ma's hairy legs, and pinched his calf—a trick she learned from my mother.

"Mmm… Ahh… Knock it off, Mimi."

"Mmm? Mmm! Aw, Mimi, you're such a nag…"

"Ow! Mimi, let me sleep! Memorize the vocab for me and I'll save a seat for you tomorrow."

And that's how Mimi improved her English.

There were bottles smashing, people whooping it up, vomiting, stomping, running and crying… those were the sounds Mimi heard in her dubious dreams. She lifted her head, yawned, and fell asleep again on her textbook.

In the dark night, crimson streams gushed from a young body and trickled down the Coastal Highway, racing with the waters of the Ma-wu-k'u. A silver blade went in, a red blade emerged, and youthful heroism was swallowed by the inky silence of the night. The wolves howled, and left to hide themselves in the mountains.

One morning, an abrupt phone call woke my family up. It was the police telling us that something had happened to A-ma, and that they needed my dad to be there.

A-ma burst into tears as soon as he saw my dad. He always cried when he saw my dad, as if he had been grievously wronged and was seeking consolation from his own father.

Several times when my father went to the police to bail him out, A-ma didn't say anything, just cried. The time he cried the hardest was when he was doing military service on one of Taiwan's small offshore islands. My father got a chance to go there and meet A-ma, whose eyes turned red as soon as he saw my father appear. When my father gave him a thousand dollars, he hugged him and burst into tears. It was so weird. I hadn't seen him so sad even when Big Daddy Dragon passed away.

On the other side of the bars, my dad saw A-ma and his companions from the neighbouring village sitting on a bench with their hands cuffed. Each of them looked pale with fear and exhaustion.

"Don't cry, A-ma. Tell me what happened," my father said. "A-ma, since your father died, I have always treated you like my own son. You have to tell me what happened."

"Uncle, it has nothing to do with me!"

Then, my father told the police about A-ma's "pathetic past" exaggeratedly, garrulously and smartly. (Later it was replayed again and again like a cassette.)

A-ma's father died when A-ma was sixteen. His mother remarried (?) another guy, turning A-ma into an orphan with a self-destructive streak. Basically a good, timid boy, A-ma turned bad when he hung with the wrong crowd. He never did any of the things he was accused of himself. He was just following others' lead, going along for the ride.

And then my father smugly told the story about A-ma being afraid of a broken water cistern when he was little. Then he laughed. "What evil can a person this timid do? What evil can a person afraid of a broken water cistern do? I knew he was cowardly and weak when he was little. His father thought that he would be a tiger son. Look at his name, Lung Chi-Ma: Dragon Unicorn-horse. Two mythical animals! What a magnificent name! But a truly great man doesn't act like this."

My dad's words made everyone laugh. Even A-ma's companions laughed. A-ma, mouth contorted, couldn't stop crying right away, but he did smile for a moment.

A-ma was brought back to the Mahjong Den by my father. Ruby had only just now woken up and realized what had taken place. "Oh my. How can so many things happen in one night?" She was astonished. "We're lucky that it was just some cuts and bruises. If someone died, maybe you would have to go to jail!" Ruby caressed A-ma's sweaty forehead and sniffed his clothes. "I said you shouldn't drink so much if you can't hold your drink. But do you listen?"

"Mrs Dragon." My father was still not used to calling Ruby by any other name. "You shouldn't let him stay at home with nothing to do all day. Wasn't he going to try to get into a college? Why don't you send him to a cram school in Taipei?"

"I told him, but I can't make him do anything if he doesn't want to. I can't get him to do anything."

A-ma became mostly taciturn. He'd sleep in, get up, eat and go back to sleep, the flab accumulating inch by inch. The more times he got arrested the less surprised people were. Even my father no longer cared. When A-ma said he wanted to use the last of his inheritance to buy a car and learn to drive a taxi my mother couldn't wait to advise Dad to liquidate the piece of land they'd bought together and give A-ma his share of the proceeds. "One less thing to worry about. If you don't give it to him now, Ruby'll think we're sitting on Big Daddy Dragon's money. I'll bet the idea to buy a car is Ruby's," she said. "If she really cares about her son, let her go talk to the police next time A-ma gets arrested. Don't come to us."

A-ma bought the car. But he spent less time driving the taxi than driving his mates around on joyrides. He got arrested for fighting or getting into trouble, and acquired an entourage of little elementary school delinquents who played truant to follow him around, serving him tea and cigarettes like he was a mafia boss. The Old Stags in the Mahjong Den were dying off, their territory taken over by these delinquents. Unable to stand the sight, Busybody Chang yelled at Chou Shih-yung: "You got a lot to be sorry for to Big Daddy Dragon, letting his son roam around free. What kind of man are you, repaying Big Daddy's kindness like this?"

"You don't know shit!" said Chou a bit sarcastically, his boozy saliva flying onto Busybody Chang. "A-ma's not even Dragon's kid! His dick got blown off in the war." He burped and started giggling. "It's buried in a poppy field in northern Burma. Ha ha. If I hadn't carried him three days and nights, he'd have given up the ghost." Chou collapsed onto Busybody Chang's diminutive frame.

Chang spluttered for quite a while before managing to speak. No wonder! No wonder Big Daddy Dragon would let Chou Shih-yung run wild. No wonder it was Chou who bathed him after he passed away.

Chou looked up and cackled. "The Dragon's old cock was a withered opium poppy. Ha ha ha."

Busybody Chang boxed his ears and said: "Then who is A-ma's father?"

"Beats me. Ruby was in the brothel so many years she can't have kids of her own. She got A-ma from a teenage prostitute."

"Blimey!" Chang grabbed his arm and opened his mouth even wider.

She got A-ma from someone else after all. Long-kept, this big secret quickly made the rounds of the village until A-ma heard it himself. By that time he wasn't particularly sad or shocked. Like when Dragon Senior died, he wasn't as upset as people had expected. People also expected he wouldn't get along well with Chou, but except for talking a bit less, you often heard him calling "Uncle", or even playing Mahjong with him. "What a weird kid!" Pappy Shou said, wagging his head.

But a week later A-ma took up his backpack and said he

was heading to Taipei. He walked along the Coastal Highway in the morning muttering: "Day in day out he tells me to go retake the mainland and dig up the gold he buried there. Turns out all that's buried there is a rotten dick."

Mumbling to himself, A-ma started crying.

This lazy bastard of a grandson A-ma has no more right to be my noble lover. Why cry for him anymore? Mimi asked. You really are something—Aye!

9. Please spare my life, Uncle

IT HAS BEEN A LONG TIME SINCE I LEFT MY HOMETOWN FOR college, and now I was finally back in this small village in a bend of the Ma-wu-k'u. Even though the village is tranquil, I was still able to observe subtle differences. Was it possible that I felt like a traveller? Now that I'd started playing the role of an observer, I'd been forcibly excluded. I felt especially excluded when the Old Stags would look me up and down from afar for ages before finally yelling out, "It's you!" Or when a pack of black, white and spotted dogs came out of nowhere and snarled at me. At moments like this I found, oh! my depression piling up like the fallen needles of the whistling pine trees.

The Mahjong Den is located east of the Coastal Highway, hidden inside the big windbreak. The Old Stags live the expatriate lifestyle of seedy veterans of the Second Sino-Japanese War and the Chinese Civil War here, where they enjoy the protection of the surrounding whistling pines. They have no given names or family names, withered as they now are. When you walk into the windbreak, you hear the liveliest ever whistling pines conversing with each other via their twigs and needles. They are so close to the sky, sharing trivial matters so happily. Listen. You have to listen carefully, to the indistinct, confusing native dialect they speak.

To the west of the Mahjong Den, you see the new tourist spots along the Ma-wu-k'u River. The spoil from the new road was poured into the limpid green river water, covering half of the pure white marble of the columns. You see crowds of tourists getting out of cars at weekends, group after group, posing stiffly like movie stars for photos and then suddenly coming to life again, tossing out fruit rinds and garbage at will. By this time, our leading man A-ma, who has become fat and useless, will be yelling at people who want to park their cars: "A hundred! A hundred! A hundred a pop!" Be careful, you better not turn a deaf ear or after you walk excitedly back from your brief tour, you'll find your beloved car scratched or dented, tyres deflated. Somewhere nearby, A-ma will still be sitting there on the white marble, cracking a smile, shaking his legs and smirking at you, like he is the protector of the realm, the local warlord. The only person A-ma is afraid of at the moment is my younger brother A-chung, who has just become a policeman. He will immediately run away as soon as he sees my brother coming over, his plump body jiggling weirdly as he runs along the Coastal Highway before disappearing into the whistling pine windbreak.

At night, he appeared in the yard. "A-chung, you're back! How is your new job?" A-ma asked. My brother A-chung did not reply. As my father looked on, gazing at my brother's big head, he recalled many years ago when cloddish little A-chung used to follow behind A-ma all the time. He gave a heartfelt sigh before whispering proudly to my mother: "Who says our little A-chung has to follow A-ma's lead?"

"Who else ever said that besides you?!" My mum always likes to pour the proverbial cold water on my father's head.

A-ma sold the taxi and started to demand money from the tourists to make sure nothing bad happened to their cars. However, this protection racket is only profitable at the weekend. During the rest of the week A-ma just wanders aimlessly in the Mahjong Den. As the Old Stags passed away one by one, A-ma replaced them with a new gang of misfit friends, who disappear whenever A-ma is in trouble. No one cares about A-ma.

A-ma's woman, Uya, disappeared after A-ma brought up the idea of going to Taipei to earn their "wedding fund". When A-ma finally came back from Taipei, the pregnant Uya was nowhere to be seen. Everyone asked this father-and-groom-to-be where she was, but he, with his Great Man's head, which had started to swell and deform, just stumbled around and said: "Beats me! We got off the train and she said she wanted to go to the toilet and never came out," with an innocent look on his face. The way A-ma answered changed according to his psychological state, as if he had already anticipated all the different possible reasons people might come up with for Uya's disappearance. "Don't worry. She wanted me to come back first and once she finishes her stuff, she'll be back." "She waited for me to come back home from work every day, but one day I got home and she wasn't there. She just disappeared without leaving any message. I looked for her for a few days but I couldn't find her."

My kid brother, A-chung, had the police sense that A-ma's claim that someone wanted to kill him was related to Uya's disappearance. However, A-ma said nothing no matter how A-chung asked him. A-ma just kept on talking about insignificant details. "Uya's good at massage, top fingers. When I met her she was working as a massage therapist in the salon. Hey, A-chung," said A-ma slapping A-chung on the back. "When I find Uya, how about I let her give you a massage?" "Oh, A-chung, did I tell you that I was once a pimp? Actually, when I was in Taipei, Uya worked in our place." "He he he, A-chung, you're still a virgin, right?"

A-chung didn't believe him. He just laughed and shrugged it off. However, when A-ma said: "A-chung, you know what, your sister Mimi used to have a crush on me," that got a rise out of him. "God! You, a match for my sister?!" he said. "When's the last time you took a good look at yourself in the mirror?"

A-chung found quite a few safe houses for A-ma. But the people he claimed were coming for him changed every time. Sometimes he said that it was Uya's brothers who wanted to kill him, sometimes it was his brothers in the gangs that he used to run with, and sometimes it was his rivals from when he made a living from the parking space protection racket. Every time they arrived in a new hiding place, A-ma would head right for the bathroom and lock himself inside for ages. Several toilet flushes later, A-chung would have no idea what he was up to. The only thing he was sure of was that A-ma was not telling the truth.

A-ma always closed the windows and doors tight and hid beside the window edge. In a nervous whisper, he would say: "They're coming… to get me!" and rush into the toilet to hide. "A-ma come out, there isn't anyone outside." "A-chung, you should find a place to hide quickly. I can hear them. They're coming." A-ma's tremulous voice.

A-chung was losing his patience listening to the sound of the toilet flushing, so he knocked on the door to tell A-ma to come out right this minute. His voice still trembling, A-ma said: "A-chung, I'm taking a crap, you know how long it takes me."

A-chung finally lost his temper listening to A-ma talk to himself. He said to the air in the empty house: "A-ma's losing it."

"Course he's losing it. After sniffing that much junk. If you could see all the white powder he dumped in the toilet—it's all his," said Mimi, standing somewhere A-chung could not see or hear.

Later A-ma finally came clean, the time he got tossed in the fishpond. Uya's burly brothers came a calling. They beat A-ma until he was black and blue, and broke his nose. A-ma knelt on the ground and pleaded for mercy. "It… it wasn't my idea. It was what Uya wanted. She said I couldn't make money fast enough, that we didn't need to have a baby now. So we got the baby taken out, she said we'll get married after she feathers our nest… Uncle, please spare my life! It's not my fault at all." No matter how many times A-ma begged for mercy, there was no avoiding the unhappy fate of getting tossed into the fishpond. As A-ma's orange blood dispersed through the pool, you could vaguely make out a skim of fatty oil floating on the surface. That day, a lot of the little carp in the pool died from the stench.

A-ma stopped going anywhere after he got tossed in the fishpond, except the whistling pine grove, where he could while away the entire day. At dinner time, Ruby would have to make the rounds of the grove shouting: "A-ma! A-maaaa! It's time for dinner!" And the echoes would curl around the branches and swoosh over the treetops. A-ma told his mother he heard the whistling pines whistling happily in the grove, conversing in that familiar dialect of his father's homeland. One day he knelt before a pine so tall it disappeared into the clouds, telling his mother, this is my father Lung Fei-yun. Then he scooted round to a few pines growing to the side and said, this is Marathon, this is Weirdo Yang, this is Chao Junior. Finally he pointed to two whistling pines and said, that'll be Pappy Shou, and that one Busybody Chang. Oh, I almost forgot, that one's going to be you.

After people die, they all become trees, A-ma told his mother.

From then on, A-ma would hang out in the grove twenty-four seven. He stripped down and ran around. The leaves that had piled up for many years crackled underfoot, and the fine needles stuck to his flabby body, becoming a kind of natural outfit. He stood straight like a whistling pine, his arms like the branches reaching up. And whenever someone lost his way in this ancient primeval grove, A-ma would strike a refined pose, grin back at the lost soul and say: "I'm a merry whistling pine."

And the one who lost his way would never walk out of the creepy maze-like grove again.

10. A letter to Mimi

DEAR MIMI, THE MA-WU-K'U IS STILL FLOWING. THE whistling pine trees continue to sprout needles, only to see them wither. My dear Mimi, please leave my world, a charmed world that seems more illusory day by day.

This is how the story started. In the maze-like windbreak, I said a great deal about the birth and background of the whistling pine trees. Perhaps he wanted to satisfy his scepticism by seeing for himself, or perhaps he was enthralled by the fantastical ambiance of my stories, but one day, my buddy Uncle Dumdum the little thief woke up in the night and explored the grove despite my repeated warnings and attempts to frighten him out of entering it alone. "I heard sounds of a ritual from a faraway land, like an invitation," he said, exhausted. After going through much trouble, we finally found Uncle Dumdum sitting miserably on a pile of cobblestones outside the windbreak. He was chewing on fallen whistling pine twigs and needles, of which traces could be found at the corners of his mouth and in the yellowish tracks of his drool. I grabbed the bottle of XO which my father had kept for years and which Uncle Dumdum had stolen from my little white house. When I swirled the bottle, I realized there was not a single drop left. Furious, I hit him on the back of his head.

"What happened, Dumdum?"

"So much happened last night..." He heaved a sigh of

relief. He smiled at us in a daze, his mouth still hanging wide open, as if he had passed through a miasmic realm and had phantasmagorical visions.

The audience were fools, and the players madmen. Dear Mimi, when I showed my friend Uncle Dumdum the little thief around my beautiful hometown, I embellished the stories surrounding the place. Who would have thought he would have ended up foolishly living in this alternative reality I had shaped through my stories?

After our visit to the east coast, he manically scribbled his masterpiece. That's the story of your birth, Mimi. He meticulously rewrote the characters and events I had made up into a dazzling piece of fiction that turned back to mock me. "You are Mimi." After I expressed my indignation, Uncle Dumdum pointed at himself and said: "How could I be Mimi?" But it was a fit of pique pure and simple. Mimi, I wonder if you still remember what I said? "That's not how it was." "I wasn't telling the truth," I muttered, talking to myself. "Mimi truly exists," I kept muttering for days on end. Mimi, you entered my cursed dream and spoke to me—this was this and that was that—putting everything into place. When I got back to where we started from, I realized I was the fool all along. In the arguments I had with you, I once arrogantly thought you both were just puppets who danced to my tune. I can't claim the moral high ground: I am no better than Uncle Dumdum. I twisted truths and spread stories. But when I discovered more about you both and entered deeper into your world, I couldn't help but meekly realize: while playing the role of a bystander, I was slowly losing my corporality. Mimi, am I your manifestation in this world? Or are you simply a pawn in my hand?

"Pfff, Mimi was nothing like that, was she?"

Just when I was about to have a meltdown, my brain about to burst, my mind clogged with tangles of thoughts, my buddies in the Celestial Retreat started commenting: "That's just the way Mimi is."

"No, no, no… Mimi's nothing like that."

Quack whack bam squawk, they began bickering like the whistling pines in the windbreak. Their words were cruder than the dialect slang terms the Old Stags were fond of using! #%^, %&^, and *^%. All worn out, I stood up and stretched my arms wide. I repeated A-ma's words: "I am a merry whistling pine tree."

Dear Mimi, the whistling pine trees still bud, only to see their needles wither, the Old Stags continue to converse happily, and my friends carry on with their intense debates. You should move on too, continue your existence in someone else's world. Please, my dear Mimi.

SHIH CHIUNG-YU was born in Taiwan in 1968. She grew up in Taitung, a village of aboriginal Taiwan. She has been a writer, essayist, news reporter and documentary filmmaker for many years. Her novel *Masked Dolls* was published by Balestier Press.

The novellas in this collection have garnered numerous accolades, including China Times Literature Award and United Daily News Literature Award.

DARRYL STERK has translated numerous short stories by Taiwanese writers for *The Taipei Chinese Pen*, *Asymptote* and *Pathlight*. His novel translation includes Wu Ming-Yi's *The Man with the Compound Eyes* and *The Stolen Bicycle*, Chang Ying-Tai's *The Bear Whispers to Me*, and Horace Ho's *The Tree Fort on Carnation Lane*. He is a Professor of Translation at Lingnan University, Hong Kong. As a scholar he works on the representation of Taiwan's indigenous peoples in film and fiction.

His translation of *The Stolen Bicycle* was longlisted for the 2018 Man Booker International Prize.

www.ingramcontent.com/pod-product-compliance
Lightning Source LLC
Chambersburg PA
CBHW032039180726
48284CB00008B/2655